$\mathcal{A}$
$\mathcal{L}$asting
$\mathcal{B}$ond

Angie Richardson

Published in the United States by JMK Publishing

Clarksville, AR 72830

ISBN: 0692616497

DEDICATION

This book is dedicated to my parents for buying the enchanted house that became the childhood home of my dreams.

Thank you for the best childhood imaginable.

Prologue

It was nearing midnight and the house was bathed in the kind of total darkness that only exists on a moonless night. Five-year-old Kelli was fast asleep in her cozy bed, but something was beckoning, calling, attempting to rouse her from a deep sleep.

She stirred again and this time she opened her eyes and briefly looked around, wondering what had interrupted her dreams and awakened her. A princess nightlight plugged into the wall outlet next to her bed beamed across the floor, washing her room in a soft, pink glow.

She lifted her head from the pillow and propped herself up on her elbows, listening intently for a moment. The silence of the night was palatable.

Still, she continued to listen and except for the occasional car driving down the nearby road, she heard nothing. Perhaps it had been a clap of distant thunder or the bark of a lonely dog. Whatever the reason, she was awake now and needed the comfort of her mother in order to return to sleep.

She slid out of bed, and her toes touched the smooth, cool planks of the hardwood floor. Quietly, she padded out of her bedroom toward the safe haven of her parents' bedroom down the hall. Quickening her pace, she rounded the doorway through the living room and stopped at the small intersection of the kitchen and hallway.

Already knowing what consistently awaited her at night in this very spot, she nonetheless slowly turned her head to the left and saw her. *Just like always.*

She stared at the approaching faceless form of a young girl dressed in navy and holding a doll—or a baby; she never could be sure which. As always, she felt no fear or danger, but paused only long enough to smile and wave before continuing her journey down the hall.

* * * * * * *

.

Bright sunbeams cheerily streamed through the window and into the small kitchen. Kelli sat at the round, wooden table eating a bowl of cereal, while her mother stood at the counter whisking eggs in a glass bowl.

"I saw her again last night," Kelli said in a conversational tone in between mouthfuls of Cheerios.

Her mother poured the eggs into a hot, sizzling skillet on the stove. "Saw who again, honey?"

"The little girl." She scooped out another spoonful of cereal and looked wide-eyed at her mother. "You know," she said, speaking slowly in an effort to fully enunciate the words, as if her mother might not completely understand her. "The same little girl I *always* see when I get up during the night."

Her mother abruptly put the spatula down and turned to study her daughter. She was slowly beginning to grasp what was taking place inside the walls of this house. She had never experienced anything like it personally, and she was far from comfortable with it, but she had no idea what to do about it.

Chapter 1
23 Years Later

Kelli Evans fumbled around in her oversized handbag for the key to the front door. It was a beautiful, mild, March morning, and she was standing under the covered front porch of her childhood home in Arkansas. She still could not believe that she actually quit her career, moved across the country and bought this treasured little home where so many happy childhood memories were made. She, along with her brother and parents, had moved from this house when she was just ten years old, but it had always retained a special place in her heart and occasionally the little house still entered her dreams at night.

The house's exterior was made up of rough-cut native stone in varying shades of brown. A high, arched roof jutted out over the small front porch. Kelli had watched her father build this covered porch which was now sagging in the middle and badly in need of a fresh coat of paint. The entire yard, which boasted well-tended flower beds when Kelli was a girl, was now a jumble of weeds, overgrown shrubs, and trees. The previous owner had left enough junk lying around to easily fill the bed of a truck and would need to be hauled to the nearest landfill.

A light breeze caressed Kelli's blonde, shoulder-length hair as she turned the key in the lock. She was tall, and dressed as she was this morning in skinny jeans, a cashmere sweater and a pair of knee-high suede boots, she looked as stylish and willowy as a fashion model.

When she stepped inside the front door, she was immediately overcome with emotion, just as she had expected to be. Her hand flew to her open mouth in an attempt to stifle a gasp and tears threatened in the corners of her eyes. She'd only been inside once since she was ten and that was the month before when a realtor had met her here. It now felt as if her mind were playing some sort of trick on her, as if she had walked into a time machine and was now a child again. As she looked around her beloved house, she saw that some things had changed, such as the removal of a wall that had separated her bedroom from the living room. The attic had also been opened up, and a black wrought-iron staircase led up to a tiny landing with a circular window that overlooked the back yard. It would be the perfect spot for a small study or library, Kelli thought, her mind spinning with creative ideas.

She still couldn't quite wrap her mind around the fact that she actually owned this house, and she reflected on the chain of events that had led her back.

Several years before, she had earned her M.B.A. and immediately began working for a large investment firm on Wall Street. Her days were long, often exceeding 15 hours, and she totally immersed herself in learning everything she could about stocks and investments. Her ambition to succeed superseded everything else in her life, and she climbed the corporate ladder swiftly and with such precision that she impressed those around her and astonished even herself. She had made quite a name for herself in the investment world, and the firm she worked for had not only tagged her as a rising leader in corporate management, but was grooming her for one of the much-coveted positions in higher management.

She had been dating a man for over three years, when there was time, for he was in a similar field, that of corporate banking. They understood each other very well, or so she had thought. Each completely comprehended the demands of the other's job. Long days were necessary, even expected, and there were always lunch or dinner meetings with clients, plus weekend work and even extended travel on occasions. Now she realized that she had illogically believed in the back of her mind that they had a future together and perhaps would even get married one day, although they had never actually discussed it.

4

In hindsight she realized that she didn't really know him at all.

One day he had come over to tell her that he was leaving because he had accepted a job offer in Paris, one that he couldn't refuse. He'd admitted to her that this job was all he had ever wanted in life, and he was sure she would be completely thrilled with this opportunity for him. He had then told her that he couldn't chance having any excess baggage that might get in his way of achieving this dream.

She only remembered sitting there with her mouth gaping open, unable to grasp that she'd just been referred to as "excess baggage."

He had gone on to say that he knew she'd understand and suggested a celebratory dinner at a fancy restaurant and a night of romance back at his place "for old time's sake."

Kelli had just stared at him in disbelief. After three years with him there was no suggestion of a life together, a move together, not even the discussion of a *future* together. That was when she did some deep soul-searching of her own and did not like what she found. When was the last time that she had even enjoyed something as simple as watching a spectacular sunset or taking a long walk in the country? It had been far too long, she'd unhappily realized.

This was when she had first entertained the crazy idea of leaving the rat race and moving back to start all over in the friendly Arkansas town where she'd spent her idyllic childhood, an idea that grew more appealing with each passing day. *What if?* became *why not?* and before she knew it she was on the internet searching for houses on the market in her hometown of Fayetteville.

She clearly remembered how her heart literally skipped a few beats when she ran across the picture of her childhood home. She quickly found the listing agent's phone number and immediately called her on the phone, heady and breathless with excitement from the possibility of living there again. The agent was obviously perplexed by Kelli's declaration that she wished to buy the house as soon as possible, sight unseen.

"It is . . . uh," faltered the realtor. "Well, it is a fixer-upper. There's some work that needs to be done to the place."

Kelli assured her that it did not matter and suggested a date that she could fly down and they could finalize the paperwork. The agent ended their conversation obviously baffled, but elated, no doubt thinking that this had been the easiest house sale in her entire career.

Kelli retrieved a notepad from her handbag and began to walk through the house, jotting down notes about work that would need to be performed. The drywall in the bathroom would need to be replaced due to a previous leak behind the tub. She envisioned gutting the whole bathroom and giving it a total modern makeover.

Next, she went into the kitchen, and instantly her mind raced back to when she was a child and sat in this very room with her family for dinner every night. She looked at the now-empty spot where the table once sat and remembered the many, festive birthday parties that had occurred inside this very room. It was so good to be back, and as she hugged her arms to her chest, a sense of contentment washed over her. She took a long, realistic look around with fresh eyes and realized the work that would need to be done to this room, as well. The linoleum flooring was yellowed and cracked in many places. The appliances, though newer than the ones that had been here when she was a girl, were mismatched and outdated. The old brown paneling that covered the walls looked tired and dreary. Kelli penciled in her ideas for this room, also.

She glanced around the room once more, and as she did so a vague memory surfaced, and a shiver suddenly and quite unexpectedly ran down her spine, causing her breath to quicken.

She cautiously walked to the middle of the room to the area where it had always occurred. Slowly, she circled, looking behind her and in front of her as the memory took form. As a child, when she would get out of bed during the night, in this very spot she would often see the form of a young girl coming to meet her. As an adult she had realized that she had undoubtedly been seeing a ghostly apparition of some sort.

Kelli had even spoken to her mother about this in the past.

Her mother had answered with a quiet acceptance, her brow furrowed. "I soon realized that you had to be seeing an apparition who appeared to no one else in the family except you. When you were barely three you mentioned seeing her for the first time." Her mother had sighed. "At first, I thought you just had an imaginary friend, like most little kids have at some point, but this went on the entire time we lived in that house. You never appeared frightened and your story was always consistent."

Footsteps outside, followed by a sharp knock at the back door near the kitchen, startled Kelli and brought her out of her reverie. She walked to the door, cautiously opened it, and stared wordlessly for what seemed like a full minute at the man standing before her with insanely grey eyes, sandy blonde hair and a dimpled, boyish face. There was something extremely familiar about this face, yet it took a few additional seconds for full recognition to register.

"Jace!" Kelli exclaimed and without hesitating, she lunged forward and threw her arms around his neck.

He enthusiastically returned her hug, lifting her briefly off the floor and swinging her around in his stout arms. Then he sat her down gently and took a step back, his eyes casually sweeping over her from head to toe.

"My, you've certainly grown up and changed from the little girl I used to know! How long has it been? Fifteen, sixteen years?" he contemplated.

Kelli was still feeling a bit disconcerted from seeing Jace as a grown man. "Let me think. We moved away when I was ten and you were twelve, so it's been about eighteen years since we've seen each other."

She was looking Jace over, her head slightly cocked to one side. "Speaking of growing up, you've certainly come a long way from being that lanky kid who, I swear, lived for the sole purpose of teasing me."

"Hey, I always thought of you as my kid sister, so I had to treat you as such." He smiled broadly showing a mouth full of such perfectly-straight, pearly teeth that he easily could have modeled for toothpaste commercials.

She took a step back, opening the door wider and motioning for him to enter. "Please, come on in," she invited. "I'm sorry I can't offer you a seat, but as you can see there is no furniture yet."

She stepped aside for him to enter and then asked, "How did you know I was back?"

Jace followed her inside to the empty kitchen. "Your returning to Fayetteville is the hot gossip around here. As you can see, it's still a small neighborhood so whenever someone new moves in, everyone finds out all they can about him. Mrs. Tanner still lives next door, and when she heard that a Kelli Evans was the new owner of this house, she called me, and together we speculated that it had to be you." Mrs. Tanner had always been like a grandmother to the neighborhood kids.

"I'm thrilled that we were right." He cast another appreciative glance her way with those penetrating grey eyes that were the color of smoke. "So, what brings you back to your hometown? Last I heard you were a big wheel on Wall Street or something like that."

Kelli laughed at his description. "I don't know about being a 'big wheel,' as you so eloquently put it, but I did work on Wall Street with a large investment firm. Work became my life, and the more hours I put in, the more that needed to be done." She looked off in the distance.

8

"Actually, I grew tired of the hectic lifestyle and realized I was missing out on simpler, more important things in life. So I decided to quit my job and move back to this town where the pace is much slower, and I have so many fond memories. When I saw that this house was up for sale, I took it as a sign that I was making the right decision." She shook her head and shrugged. "So, here I am, the new owner of my childhood home which, I might add, has fallen into gross disrepair since my family lived here."

Jace crossed his arms and leaned back against the doorframe, his long legs stretched out in front of him. "This house has never been cared for since your family left it. There have been numerous owners, some structural changes, but no one has cared for the yard or simply painted the porch in years. Even the roof looks like it might not survive the next storm. You definitely have your work cut out for you."

"My family thinks I've lost my mind," Kelli replied as she gazed around the kitchen. "Mother still cannot understand why I gave up a very prosperous career to come back to this little place in order to start over."

"You can't live your own life trying to live up to someone else's expectations," Jace replied. "You have to choose what makes you content. Otherwise you simply travel through life a very unhappy person."

Kelli nodded in agreement, wondering if he was speaking from personal experience. She noticed again what a striking man Jace had grown to become. "What about you? What do you do now?" Sadly, their families had pretty much lost touch with one another over the years.

Before he could reply, his cell phone rang, and he excused himself as he retrieved it from the pocket of his jeans. "Dr. Harrison," he answered, stepping into the small mudroom off of the kitchen.

Kelli stared after him in disbelief. "Well, I guess that answers my question," she muttered under her breath.

Chapter 2

"**Y**ou're a doctor?" Kelli asked Jace in astonishment after he had finished his brief conversation and was sticking his phone back into the pocket of his jeans.

"Cardiologist. And why do you act so surprised? After all, we used to pretend like we were driving ambulances while riding our bikes when we were kids . . . or don't you remember?" He was smiling at her in a playful way.

"Of course I remember. Your father's old toolshed in your backyard was the hospital as I recall," she said laughing. "But, now . . . you . . . I mean, you're a real . . . ."

Jace was chuckling at her as he hurried out the door. "I'm sorry that I have to leave, but I've got an emergency at the hospital. It was great to see you again, and we'll get together soon," he promised, as he sprinted across the patio and into the yard, waving goodbye.

Kelli stood at the back door watching him jog back to wherever he had come from. She watched as he headed back across the street toward the house his family used to live in. Did he live in his childhood home as well? They had so much to catch up on, she realized.

She went back inside and concluded jotting down ideas and the necessary repairs in her notebook and then decided to return to the apartment in town which she was renting while this house was being renovated. She had purchased a local newspaper that morning which, along with the internet, should give her an idea of where to start regarding hiring a carpenter.

She spent most of the afternoon making calls to various carpenters, crossing names off the list of those who were too busy to begin her job anytime in the near future. By the end of the afternoon she had narrowed the list of names to three and would meet them individually at the house tomorrow to get their estimates.

That evening as she was preparing for bed, Kelli found herself thinking back to Jace and the warm feeling of seeing him again, after so many years spent apart. He had grown into a strikingly handsome man, rugged in a sense, but yet with the same boyish face of his childhood, although it was more angular now. And those eyes of his were like pools of molten lead, yet now they exuded depth and maturity.

He had been as a brother to her in their childhood, a friend across the road to play with during the long summer days of their youth. They had once shared normal childhood activities together such as fishing, biking, games of tag and catching fireflies at dusk on summer evenings. She had even given in to playing war with Jace and her brother, and in turn, they had played dolls with her. Except, back then it wasn't called anything as girlie as "playing with dolls." It was given a more masculine name, like "Steal the Baby," and there had been imaginary cops and detectives involved.

Jace was a monumental piece of her having such an idyllic childhood, she realized. He was in nearly every memory of living here. It was a little disarming to see him now as a man and how attractive he'd become. And a doctor! Not just a doctor, but a cardiologist! Kelli didn't know why, but this revelation had stunned her beyond words. It's not that he wasn't intelligent, for she had known that he was a smart kid, but it was just hard to believe that her playmate was now a man who had a very important job saving lives. He had certainly made a success of his life.

The next morning, Kelli awoke early, dressed and ate breakfast. She was anxious to return to the house and get started on the work. The three prospective carpenters were meeting her there throughout the day to survey the job and write up estimates. In the meantime there were things that she could begin to do herself, such as pulling up the old carpet and linoleum.

But once she arrived at the house, she noticed again how disheveled the entire yard and entry looked. It promised to be a glorious day outside, so she decided to tackle the yard rather than work inside. She had worn old clothes and brought a pair of work gloves, knowing that she would need them. As she glanced down at her pants and long-sleeved t-shirt, she had to laugh thinking that her attire this morning was such a far cry from that of her working days. Yet not having to conform to a dress code also felt like a freedom that she had not experienced in a long time.

Kelli spent the majority of the day piling old boards onto a burn pile, raking leaves, and pruning heavily overgrown shrubs. She had to cut away twisted, ropy vines of honeysuckle before even being able to reach the shrubs growing beneath them. The muscles in her arms ached tremendously from not being used this way in years. She panted and sweated and pulled, yet admitted that it felt wonderful.

The carpenters had each shown up, as promised, and Kelli had led them around the house, referring to her notes about what needed to be done and her ideas of the way that the finished rooms should look. The first guy seemed overwhelmed with her ideas and the job, saying it would take much too long, and he couldn't spend the required amount of time on the project. The other two men were both interested in the job and left saying they would be submitting an estimate to her sometime during the week.

By late afternoon, Kelli had felt like much had been accomplished in the day, and she was sitting outside on the back steps, drinking a bottle of water, when she spotted Jace walking across the backyard toward her. He was wearing a red Razorback t-shirt and faded jeans which accentuated his long legs.

"Mind if I join you?" he asked, motioning to the steps.

Kelli scooted over, happy to see him. "It looks like one of the first things I need to buy is a patio set with comfortable seating," she said smiling. She subconsciously pushed a strand of hair from her eyes and attempted to brush off the thick layers of dirt from her pants.

"Busy day saving lives?" she asked.

Jace groaned. "It's always busy. There's never much slack time when it comes to other people's lives. Since receiving that phone call yesterday, I've been at the hospital until about an hour ago. I was actually about to crash in bed, but I looked out the window and saw you sitting outside."

He surveyed the yard and the heaping burn piles. "Looks like you've accomplished a lot yourself. Did you have any help with this?" he asked, nodding toward tall piles of pruned brush and cut limbs.

"No. A couple of carpenters came today to look around, and they've promised to write up estimates, but I've done all this alone. I didn't plan on working outside, but it was such a beautiful day, and when I arrived I noticed how awful the house appeared from the road. So much of getting this place back in shape is just cleaning up."

She let out a long sigh and leaned her aching back against the door frame. "In all honesty, it felt terrific to actually do some decent physical work again, although I may not be able to get out of bed in the morning."

Jace laughed. "Say, tomorrow is my day off, although I will be on call. How about I meet you over here and help? We still have lots of catching up to do."

Kelli stared at him. "Are you sure that you want to spend a valuable day off doing this kind of manual labor? Wouldn't you rather be doing something fun?"

"I consider manual labor a wonderful reprieve from my normal job. It keeps me grounded and it's a wonderful diversion. I'd really like to help, if you wouldn't mind it."

"Well, if you're absolutely sure. And I'd love for you to come over. By the way, do you still live in your childhood home?" She had assumed that he did since she saw him walking across the road from that direction again.

"I currently do. But I'm beginning the tedious process of building a new one on the hill behind it. Right now they are still just working on the foundation, and there is not anything that I can help with at this point." He pulled himself up to his full height and took a step, then stopped. "I'll show it to you sometime if you'd like. Well, I'll see you here tomorrow, ready to work."

Kelli hoisted her aching body to an upright position. "I'd love to see your house site, Jace." She paused. "By the way, I've not even asked, but do you have a family? I mean, are you married?"

"No," his grin spread slowly. "Like you, I've not found the right person yet."

Kelli felt her face flush under his scrutiny. "What makes you think I haven't found the right person?" she asked indignantly.

"You're not wearing a ring," Jace replied taking a step toward the backyard. "Also, no offense, but I can't see some big-city guy eagerly moving to this place, leaving behind a fancy job and equally fancy sky-rise apartment." She caught the wink he tossed her way. "Just saying." He began walking across the yard in long strides. "I'll bring my pruners tomorrow," he called over his shoulder and then disappeared across the road.

Kelli could see the roofline of the house where Jace was raised and where he currently lived, but the oak trees lining his drive and front yard had grown so tall and full over the last 20 years that the actual house was not visible from where she sat. Still, he had said that he looked out his window and saw her in the back yard, so there had to be some clearing among the trees somewhere.

She had to admit that she was a little unsettled about the way he had sized up her private life in such a short time. The fact that he had noticed that she didn't wear any kind of a ring showed that he was checking her out. There was certainly a lot to catch up on, she thought, as she carefully rose and dragged her aching body back into the house. She was ready to head to her apartment, soak her tired bones in a hot bubble bath, and collapse into bed.

For all she knew, she wouldn't even be able to stand on her wobbly, sore legs tomorrow, much less accomplish more yard work.

Chapter 3

T he next morning Kelli opened her eyes to a still mostly-dark room, but out of her bedroom window she could see the first light of day beginning to wash the eastern sky in pink tones. It was still very early, and she stretched out her arms and legs while still in bed, testing for any muscle soreness. Much to her surprise, she couldn't detect anything that felt out of sorts and upon rising discovered that she was only slightly stiff.

After a hot shower she fixed a hearty breakfast of scrambled eggs, bacon and toast, figuring she would need the extra calories for all the physical work she would be doing that day. She decided to pack a sandwich for lunch and then thought it would be a nice gesture to pack an extra one for Jace, if he did actually show up to help her. She felt guilty that he would be spending his day off pruning and working outdoors with her, but she hadn't asked him for any assistance, and he seemed to have his mind set on helping her.

At the house, Kelli had just begun gathering all the yard tools and deciding which area to conquer first, when Jace approached wearing faded, ripped jeans and a well-worn sweatshirt. He was waving a pair of pruners in his hand.

"Good morning. I told you I was coming armed today," he said to her as he walked up. "I thought I would whip the holly hedge along the side of the house back into shape, unless you have somewhere else that needs attention first." He was standing beside her and Kelli suddenly felt her face flush from his close proximity.

She tucked a loose strand of hair behind her ear. "Jace, you really don't have to spend your day working over here. I feel guilty."

"You don't want my help?" he questioned, one eyebrow swiftly arching over those molten gray eyes as he searched her face.

"Oh, no, it's not that. It's just . . . . "

"Look, if I didn't want to help, I certainly wouldn't be over here." He licked his lips, paused. "I have an idea. Why don't we first walk over to Mrs. Tanner's house next door? She has been so excited about your moving back to be her neighbor again. If we go now, we won't have to worry about becoming too filthy to set foot in her house later today."

"That's a great idea. I was planning on visiting her today, anyway."

They put down their garden tools and walked through the side yard toward Mrs. Tanner's house. There was still no fence between the two properties, and Kelli suddenly felt like she and Jace were eight and ten years old again, following the once well-used, but now overgrown path that led to her house. Jace led the way, ducking under low-lying limbs and holding branches back so that they wouldn't hit Kelli in the face.

"It looks like we need to clear this path to Mrs. Tanner's yard. I have a feeling that it will be used frequently again now, although it probably won't be for getting a cold glass of milk and tasting her freshly-baked cookies," Jace said as he knocked at the back door.

"That's still a wonderful reason to check on her every day," Kelli joked.

The white back door swung open, followed by the creaky screen door, and then Mrs. Tanner appeared in the doorway as a huge grin spread over her ageless face which was framed with soft, white curls. She epitomized the ultimate granny, complete with a pastel housedress, over which a ruffled apron was tied around her ample waistline. The smell of cinnamon and apples wafted from inside her house, along with the familiar aroma of lemon oil—the same comforting smell that Kelli was always met with whenever she visited Mrs. Tanner as a child. Kelli felt as if she had truly come home.

She clutched her chest and then extended her arms in welcome. "My kids are back!" she exclaimed joyfully, as she hugged Kelli's neck and pulled her closer. "Child, look at you! You've gone and grown up and become a gorgeous woman." She stepped back and held Kelli at arm's length. "Isn't she just gorgeous, Jace?"

Kelli noticed that Jace seemed a bit uncomfortable, but was nodding and smiling in agreement.

Mrs. Tanner looked up at Jace. "Seeing you two together now as adults is almost more than my little, old mind can handle. You should both still be riding your bikes down the road and stopping in for a cold soda on a hot afternoon."

Kelli hugged Mrs. Tanner tightly and felt like it was as if she were hugging a long-lost grandma. In a sense, she had come home for real. Mrs. Tanner had always been there for the neighbor kids, whether they needed a cool drink, a snack, or even a band aid. It was wonderful growing up in such a tightly-knit neighborhood, and Kelli was thankful that parts of it were still here.

They followed Mrs. Tanner into the kitchen where she offered them mugs of fresh, hot coffee, as they all sat down around her kitchen table. A plate of sugar cookies was sitting in the middle of the table.

Mrs. Tanner spoke first as she sipped her coffee and looked at Kelli. "When I heard that a girl with your name planned to buy the house next door, I tried not to get too excited hoping that it was you. Then I told Jace, and he began hearing stories from people in town about you, and we put our heads together and decided that it just *had* to be you."

She stirred more cream into her coffee as she continued. "I heard that after you graduated from college, you went on to become a very successful investor up North. Why, it sounded as if one day you would be running the entire investment company! So, what made you decide to move back to Arkansas?"

Kelli smiled at the picture which Mrs. Tanner painted. She had forgotten how quickly news traveled around small towns. "I missed home . . . you know . . . small town life. My days were one big blur, and all I saw besides my computer screen were concrete sidewalks and skyscrapers." She looked from Jace to Mrs. Tanner. "There is no grass, fields, mountains nor fresh air when you live in a large city."

She shrugged. "One day I realized that my life was passing too quickly, and I was feeling terribly unfulfilled. After some serious soul searching, I realized that I longed for a life with some substance to it."

Kelli took a sip of her coffee while Jace and Mrs. Tanner sat watching her intently, waiting for her to continue. "Imagine my excitement when I saw my old childhood home on the market one day while surfing the internet in search of homes in this area for sale. I immediately took that as a sign that moving back here was the right thing to do." She looked from Jace to Mrs. Tanner, who was smiling broadly and nodding her head vigorously in agreement.

"I believe in fate, Kelli. Your returning here was meant to be, and I am so thrilled to have you back next door to me, after all these years." She reached across the table and clasped Kelli's hands in her own.

"The old house has never looked the same since your family left. Your parents always kept it so spiffed up with fresh paint and maintained the most beautiful flower beds that I've ever seen. The owners who moved in after your family did some remodeling and kept things up, but soon afterward they moved, and the place just kept changing hands with some rather unsavory-looking people coming and going."

They spent the next hour catching up on each other's lives and family before Jace eventually scooted his chair back and stood up, holding his hand out for Kelli. "I'm sorry, Ms. Kelli, but I promised to help you with yard work today. If we don't get started it will be dinner time, and we'll still be sitting here at Mrs. Tanner's kitchen table reminiscing over old times."

Mrs. Tanner smiled at the thought. "I see nothing wrong with that. I could cook up some hearty supper, and we'd all three sit here and continue our conversation. Lord knows we still have so much to talk about. We'll do that sometime, okay?"

Jace leaned down to kiss her on the cheek. "It's a date. You just let us know what day would be good for you, and we'll both be glad to bring our appetites for some home cooking, right Kelli?"

Kelli agreed and hugged Mrs. Tanner goodbye, as she and Jace walked to the back door. As they wound their way through the shrubbery and dodged low tree limbs on the way back to Kelli's property, Mrs. Tanner stood in her doorway watching them. She couldn't help but think what an attractive couple they made as adults.

Kelli was very impressed with Jace's swiftness at pruning the side hedge, handling the pruners with such agility and adeptness that she teased him that the reason he was so good at the job was that he practiced on his heart patients all the time. By early afternoon they had added a considerable stack of debris to the brush pile, and Kelli insisted that they take a break and eat the sandwiches that she had packed that morning for them. They sat on the back steps and ate while surveying the yard.

"It seems like just yesterday that we were running around this back yard with your sister and my brother, playing tag and catching fireflies at dusk," Kelli said wistfully in between bites of her sandwich.

"Yes, it does." He pointed to the large oak at the edge of the back yard. "Do you remember when we were climbing that tree over there, and you insisted on me catching you when you jumped off the bottom limb?"

Kelli rolled her eyes at the memory. "How could I ever forget? I landed so hard on you that we both fell down, and you had a limp for a week after that little incident."

Jace rubbed his knee at the thought. "What about the time you tried to do a wheelie on your bike after you watched me do one first? You

20

crashed, landed on the gravel road, and had two bloody knees and a scraped elbow."

"Perhaps living across the road from me helped in your decision to become a doctor," Kelli retorted. They were silent for a moment, reliving old memories, and then she remarked, "Life was a lot simpler then, wasn't it?"

"Certainly was," Jace replied. "All we had to worry about was what time to be home for lunch, dinner or the requisite Popsicle in the middle of a hot afternoon. Summer days were for nothing but fun in the sun. Families seemed to have more time then, more mothers stayed home with the kids, and there were no video games to keep kids inside."

Kelli held her water bottle up to Jace's. "Here's to having had the best childhood imaginable."

"Cheers," Jace answered, his plastic bottle clinking against hers. "Now tell me some more about yourself. Are you currently seeing anyone?"

Jace's question caught Kelli completely off guard, and she quickly looked over at him. His striking, flint-grey eyes were boring into hers with such intensity that she had to glance away before answering.

"No, I'm not. I was in a long-term relationship that I assumed was leading somewhere, but my boyfriend at the time received an overseas job offer and didn't think twice about taking it without even discussing it with me. No, 'will you marry me and come with me?' Or, 'I'm considering taking this job, what do you think?' It was just goodbye and I know how thrilled you must be for me." Kelli sat the bottle down beside her, perhaps a little too hard, because some water sloshed out over the top and onto the step.

"The truth is I was too busy myself to have much time for a relationship. We basically just spent time together on the weekends.

21

When I look back on our relationship, we really didn't know each other that well at all."

Jace reached over and brushed her cheek with his fingertips, a starkly simple and innocent gesture, yet it somehow felt remarkably intimate. "I'm sorry." He sounded like he genuinely meant it.

"Thanks," Kelli said, her eyes again meeting his probing ones for an instant. She was uncomfortable talking about her previous love life with Jace and was eager to steer the subject away from herself. "What about you? Why hasn't a tall, handsome cardiologist like yourself been snatched up by now?" Then, a thought quickly entered her mind. "Or are you involved with someone?"

Jace continued staring into Kelli's eyes. Her long, blonde hair being ruffled by the gentle breeze did not go unnoticed by him, nor did the way her full, sensuous lips looked when she spoke. "I'm not seeing anyone at the moment." He shifted on the steps, looking across the road, toward his house. "Truth is a doctor's life doesn't leave much time for romance. I'm on call most days and nights. During medical school I had tough classes that required tons of studying which left little time for dating. Then, during my residency the hours were grueling, and most nights I was lucky to grab even a couple hours of sleep. "

"Your parents must be extremely proud of you, Jace. By the way, where are they now?"

"When dad retired, they decided to fulfill his dream of living out West, and so they moved to Montana. That was about six years ago. Just wait until I tell them that you have moved back into your childhood home." Jace clasped his hands between his knees before continuing. "You know, Mom always thought the world of you."

"The feeling was mutual. In fact, it was like we were all related somehow. She was always available in a pinch if something came up, and Mom had to leave. Likewise, you and your sister were always at our

22

home if your mom needed a babysitter for a short while. Our families were always there for each other.

Jace stretched his long legs out before him and reached over to pat Kelli's hand. "That's why it is so easy to see you again and to just be myself with you. You already know me." He looked over at her, his eyes framed by thick, dark lashes. "However, it is a little perplexing to see you as a woman and not as a little girl wearing pig tails and sporting skinned knees." No more than a few seconds passed, yet Kelli noticed the brief hesitancy before he spoke. "You've grown into a beautiful woman, Kelli."

Kelli opened her mouth to respond, but found that her tongue would not work. Jace had become an extremely handsome man, and it was more than a tad awkward to recall all their escapades as kids growing up together now that she looked at this gorgeous, talented, intelligent cardiologist sitting beside her. So she simply smiled at him, feeling the color rising in her cheeks. She excused herself, saying that she needed more water and went inside to the kitchen for a refill. When she returned outside, Jace was in the yard getting ready to burn the brush piles. The entire front and side yard looked infinitely better, and Kelli found herself wishing that she had thought to take "before" and "after" pictures to keep as a reminder.

By the end of the afternoon the piles were burned, and Jace and Kelli reeked of smoke and large smudges of dirt covered their shirts. But all their hard work had paid off since a person could now see the front porch from the street, and the shrubs around the front and side of the little rock house were neatly trimmed—probably for the first time in years. She looked over at Jace who was raking dirt over the last smoldering embers of the remaining brush pile.

"If I had planned this a little better, we could have roasted hot dogs and eaten s'mores for dinner as these piles burned. How can I thank you for all the work you've done for me today?" Kelli asked, walking over to stand beside him.

23

Jace leaned on the handle of the rake and faced her squarely. "I suppose you could start by agreeing to have dinner with me this weekend."

Kelli looked at him sheepishly. "I believe you've got that all wrong. I should be cooking dinner for you, instead."

"Please," Jace continued. "It would be an honor if you would accept."

Kelli looked up at his face, all the sweat and dirt from the day's work shining on his brow.

"Well, if you put it like that, how can I resist?"

"Great. How about Friday night, say 8:00? And I'll need your cell number so that I can call you for directions to your apartment."

Kelli gave him her number, and then they finished putting all the tools away. Jace was getting ready to head back to his house, but first he walked over to her, put his hands on her shoulders and ever so sweetly, so softly, murmured, "It's so great to have you back, Kel."

Kel. He had called her 'Kel.' That had been his pet name for her as a kid, and she hadn't been called it since. She melted upon hearing the name again and knew at that instant that she had better tread ever so carefully around this man.

Chapter 4

A lot of progress was made the next week on the house. Both carpenters had submitted their bids, and Kelli made her selection after checking their references. Walter Mills began work on Thursday and spent the whole day tearing down the sheetrock wall in the bathroom that had been subjected to water damage, as well as removing the worn-out tub and toilet. Kelli met with him on the design aspect of the room, and it was agreed that a walk-in tile shower would fit nicely in the corner. A new pedestal sink and toilet would complete the room, and Kelli was planning to have the floor laid in tile to match the shower.

Each day Kelli performed tasks that she could do such as tearing out the cracked and worn kitchen linoleum and pulling the filthy brown carpeting from the other rooms. To her utter delight, the beautiful hardwood floor that she remembered as a child lay beneath the carpet in the living room and was in pristine condition. She decided to locate a hardwood floor finisher and have it restored to its original beauty. When she was in the hardware store that afternoon a clerk gave her the name of someone who could do just that.

Jace stopped by late Thursday afternoon for just a few minutes. He was on his way back to the hospital. Kelli was in an old sweatshirt, jeans and her hair, which was loosely piled on top of her head, was falling down all around her face. She self-consciously tried to smooth back some fly-away pieces while tugging at her dirty sweatshirt.

Jace smiled at her appearance. She was a hard worker and certainly not afraid of getting her hands a little dirty, a trait he admired. "Just seeing that we are still on for tomorrow night," he verified.

"Of course! I've been doing hard, physical labor all week just to ensure that I'll have worked up a hearty appetite in your honor," she said smugly.

She may have felt totally lacking of beauty at this moment, but that was certainly not the case in Jace's mind. She had a beauty about her that did not need cosmetics nor styled hair to shine through.

"Great, I'll see that you follow through on that promise. I thought we'd eat at that new, little Italian restaurant downtown, if that sounds all right with you."

"Wonderful. See you tomorrow evening, Jace," she said as he left.

Friday morning proved to be a very hectic one. Kelli shopped at various home improvement stores in an attempt to choose the bathroom tile. She ended up going to a tile specialty store, and there she found exactly what she was looking for: large, beige, square tiles with a dark chocolate and soft, sage green swirl pattern. She chose a coordinating sage green smaller tile to line the shower and chair rail around the wall. The tiles would have to be ordered and shipped, but that was fine since a new wall was being rebuilt and a lot of structural work needed to be done first. She shared the finding with Mr. Mills who had been working in the house all morning. He needed a few items from town, so Kelli offered to go pick them up so that he could continue with the work he was doing. While she was at the lumber yard she set up an account for all the lumber and other items that she would need to be shipped to the worksite. These errands took the better part of the day, but she did stay and work with Mr. Mills until around five that evening when she suggested that they finish for the day. He would not be able to work the next day on the house as he and his wife had made prior plans to visit their grandkids, so it would be Monday morning before he returned.

Kelli drove to her apartment and ran a hot bubble bath. She reclined in the tub wondering what she was going to wear on her date with Jace. *Date!* She thought, laughing to herself. It really wasn't a date . . . it was just a dinner that they were going to share. They had not really had a chance to visit with each other aside from the time they did as they were working in the yard. She dried off, wrapped herself in a towel, and applied makeup. Next she dried her hair and used the curling iron to define the curls framing her face. She dabbed a light, fruity perfume on her pulse points and went to stand in front of her closet. She considered several different outfits, but settled on a light green sweater which matched her eyes, a pair of beige slacks, and beige pumps—thinking this choice was neither too dressy nor too casual.

True to his word, Jace knocked on the door at a couple minutes till eight. Kelli checked the mirror one last time for a final check of her hair and then went and opened the front door. Jace was standing there dressed in a moss-green, plaid shirt with a khaki-colored sweater tied loosely around his shoulders. Kelli was used to seeing him in a sweatshirt or scrubs, and she had to admit that he looked like he belonged on the cover of *GQ* magazine.

Meanwhile, he stood speechless as his eyes roamed over Kelli, taking in her golden curls and svelte figure which was accentuated by her sweater and form-fitting slacks. He managed to find his voice through the sudden fog in his head. "My gosh." His eyes were transfixed on Kelli. "You look absolutely amazing tonight."

His sincerity and the look on his face made Kelli blush, much to her dismay. She wasn't usually the blushing type, but a competent woman with the ability to conduct board meetings in conference rooms with lots of high-level executives. None of that, however, had ever made her feel as nervous as she did at this moment. What was it about this guy?

She willed herself to keep it together and smiled, looking into Jace's eyes. "Thank you. You don't look half-bad yourself. I'd say it's a definitive improvement over that dirty sweatshirt you had on last Saturday." She grabbed her purse, and they headed outside to a bright red, shiny BMW parked in her driveway.

"My, we certainly are going in style tonight. This car's a beauty," Kelli said appreciatively, as she ran her fingertips over the glossy hood.

Jace had a pretend look of hurt on his face. "Are you saying that you like this car better than the shiny, red bike that I received for Christmas when I was ten?" He held up his hand to stop her from saying anything. "Before you answer, may I remind you that you called it your 'dream vehicle' and begged me to let you ride it every day for an entire month?"

"Not at all," smiled Kelli. "And I'm glad to see that your color choice has remained the same. It's just that my preferred mode of transportation nowadays has changed from that of the two-wheel variety to those with four-wheels." She tossed her mane of blonde hair over her shoulder and tried to sound dignified. "It's just that I've matured, is all."

Jace couldn't resist. "I'll say you have," he said in a suggestive, taunting tone as he opened the car door for her.

The restaurant was nestled downtown on a busy street that was popular with the local university students. There were many restaurants, bars, bookstores and specialty shops lining the bustling sidewalks. Since it was a balmy spring evening, the waiter led them to a second floor, open-air terrace which provided a lovely view of the Ozark Mountains in the distance. Large, potted palms in terra cotta pots were strategically placed around the terrace, while twinkling white lights were strung on the wrought iron railing. The establishment, although newly opened, boasted a lively, eclectic crowd tonight.

As soon as they were seated, an older couple walked by and the gentleman stopped beside Jace and patted him on the back. "Good evening, Dr. Harrison," he said.

"Mr. Burns, it is so nice to see you," Jace replied, offering a handshake. "You are looking well tonight."

"Thanks to you," the elderly man replied and then he turned his attention toward Kelli. "Dr. Harrison saved my life. He performed open-

28

heart surgery on me a few months ago, and I wouldn't be here tonight if it weren't for him."

Jace patted his hand, and they shared a few more pleasantries before the couple left.

Kelli studied his face. "Your job must be so rewarding and fulfilling to you. It's awesome to think that you save lives."

Jace removed the lemon wedge from the rim of his glass and took a sip of water. "It is very fulfilling, and at times challenging, as well as exhausting. For instance, tonight I'm on call, although I'm betting that we can have a fine dinner together before an emergency happens. As a matter of fact, this is my weekend to be on call. It's part of the job."

The waiter came over and they gave him their orders. They talked about each other's families as they ate their salad and found that they truly had so much to catch up on that they were never at a loss for words. They felt comfortable with each other since they had been such close friends long ago. Granted, a lot of time had passed; but real friends have a lasting bond that transcends time and even after being apart, they still feel comfortable with one another.

They were sharing coffee and cherry cheesecake when Jace asked Kelli if she missed the idea of having a regular job and normal working hours now that she didn't have a job. She said she didn't miss the stress at all, although it was still difficult to not wake up to a screeching alarm clock and begin the day at a harried pace.

"I don't mean to pry, but how will you get income to renovate and live on? I mean, sooner or later won't you need a paycheck again?"

Kelli found humor in watching him squirm as he tried to politely navigate around this delicate question. "Naturally, I've made lots of investments since I worked in the industry. So, there is somewhat of an income in that respect in the form of dividends."

She took a sip of her drink before continuing. "However, I've also recently made a sizeable investment in something new that, hopefully, could pay off in the future." She sat her glass down and looked Jace straight in the eyes. "Have you ever heard of arabechia?"

"Of course," Jace replied, enjoying a forkful of creamy cheesecake. "As a matter of fact, I have a current medical journal on my desk right now that touts it as a promising natural medicine in the future." He closed his eyes to aid in his recollection. "It is thought to slow the growth of certain cancers, perhaps even destroy some types of cancer cells. Of course, it is too premature to conclude anything yet, but early testing shows promising results."

He looked across the table at Kelli who was listening quietly and had a serious expression on her face. "What has arabechia got to do with you?"

"As you know, it is an herb that is native to certain countries, mainly Africa," she waited for his acknowledging nod before continuing. "And you know that vast amounts are needed to harvest for experimental purposes in labs here in the United States, as well as in other countries," she said.

Jace carefully put his fork down and clasped his hands in front of him on the table, giving Kelli his full attention.

"Well," she began and then glanced down at the napkin that she was squeezing in in her lap. "I've previously studied a lot about this herb, realizing its importance and potential. So, rather than simply buying stock in some company that plans to harvest this herb, I actually went directly to the source." Her eyes met Jace's. "Meaning I bought an arabechia farm in a small settlement in Zambia."

Jace, who had her rapt attention, could no longer conceal his astonishment and his eyes grew as large as saucers. "You own a farm in Zambia?" he repeated. "How in the world did you manage to do that, what with all the language barriers, the immense distance, the cultural differences and all that goes along with that?"

"I did my homework," Kelli answered easily, as if she had merely purchased a new piece of furniture after much consideration. "I've always been good at research, so I did lots and lots of it. It is an existing 80-acre farm, which means that I won't have to hire men to plant crops again for a year, and it sits in a village called Mambashaiu, which is settled in the Zambezi River basin. Harvesting employs local men, which provides money for food to feed their families. The herbs are harvested, dried and packaged at a nearby processing plant and then shipped overseas."

Jace was visibly impressed with the ambition, goal and initiative of his treasured friend. She was obviously no slacker and had made the necessary investments to allow her to live her dreams—all of them— including quitting her job, purchasing and renovating her childhood home, and even chasing a new dream in a faraway land.

He took a drink and swallowed. "You're quite a woman, did you know that?" He said this as more of a statement than a question.

"Anyone could have done the exact same thing, Jace," she said, dismissing the compliment with a wave of her hand. "I'm just foolish enough to follow through with some of my crazy ideas. It's a gamble, and I may lose the farm, so to speak, but it's a chance that I'm prepared to take." She paused for a slight moment before continuing. "It's important for me to live my life without any regrets or 'I should-haves.'"

Jace reached over and took her hand in his. This unassuming gesture carried warmth and even admiration, but it also conveyed something else as a fiery spark coursed through her veins. Jace must have felt it too, because he quickly pulled his hand back and cleared his throat.

"How about I take you over and show you my house site? It's dark, but I have a flashlight, and you can borrow a pair of my boots."

Kelli giggled at the thought of traipsing around the hillside in the dark while wearing Jace's man-sized boots.

Twenty minutes later they were back at Jace's house. It was as if Kelli had stepped into a time machine and traveled back 20 years. Upon walking in the kitchen door, she was reminded of all the many times she had walked into this same room as a child. Not much had changed that she remembered, except new curtains were hung on the window over the sink, and the walls had been painted a soft, creamy yellow. Even the kitchen table and four chairs in the middle of the room were the same. Kelli commented on this as she whirled around, taking it all in.

"Mom and Dad left most of the furniture here when they moved. If Dad was getting to realize his dream of moving out West, then Mom said she was going to realize her dream of having new furniture," laughed Jace. "So, lucky me, I had a fully-furnished house to move into."

He led Kelli into the living room off to the right of the kitchen, and it too appeared the same way that Kelli had remembered it. "Oh, Jace," she said. "You don't know how nice it is to walk into a place that evokes such fond memories. I feel like a girl again in this house!"

"Come on, let's get you some boots to wear before you start asking to pull out the bikes and dolls to play with," teased Jace, as he opened the front coat closet and pulled out a pair of extra-large rubber boots. "These should fit you just fine. And the green will even match your sweater," he added with dancing mischief in his eyes.

"Smart-aleck," cracked Kelli. But she secretly enjoyed his humor and sharp wit.

"These are huge!" she said, holding up the boots. She pulled them on and stood up feeling like a clown in a carnival as she tried to walk in them.

"Here, hold my hand," offered Jace, and immediately upon taking his hand, she felt that fiery current run between their hands and into her body again. There was no denying that some sort of strong chemistry radiated between them.

He grabbed a flashlight and held open the door for her, leading the way through the backyard and the back pasture, pointing his flashlight on the ground as they navigated around protruding rocks. It was pitch dark outside as they made their way up the small hillside to the spot that Jace had chosen for his house.

Soon, Jace stopped and pointed the flashlight so that its beam revealed a poured foundation and some boards that were beginning to define rooms. "They've just begun framing," he explained. "Here, let me take you through the front door."

Kelli was laughing as she let him pull her up on the concrete and through an imaginary front door. He may now be a respected cardiologist, but down deep he was the same fun, happy-go-lucky little boy that she remembered. Here he was leading her up a hillside in total darkness to show her his chosen building site. It reminded her of one of their many carefree, youthful adventures.

Jace led her through what little floor plan was there, explaining that he wanted a huge window in the kitchen above the sink that would look out over his old home place. He also was adamant about having lots of windows facing west in the living room so that he would be able to view the sunset over the Ozark Mountains. Kelli couldn't help but think of how she had missed those sunsets while living and working up North.

"The builders have to pull off of this project to return to another one they've got a deadline on. They won't be able to return for several weeks, but that's okay with me because I'm really in no hurry. I have a roof over my head and I'm gone a lot anyway."

They both stood there for a few minutes looking out over the twinkling lights of town that lay before them. It was a stunning site for a house and she told him so.

"You, if anybody, would appreciate this site, Kelli. It is the very spot where we spent so many of our adventures. Do you remember fishing in the pond to the left of here?"

"Of course!" Kelli gushed. "I loved to fish, but I didn't like to bait the hook with those slimy, wiggly worms you would always bring in a bucket."

Jace smiled at the memory. "As I recall, you never had to worry about touching the slimy things because you made me always bait your hooks for you."

"That's right. I never understood why you wouldn't let me use one of those pretty, pastel-colored, feathery lures in your tackle box on my line instead. They were much more attractive."

Jace was laughing out loud now. He reached over and in one quick maneuver, pulled her against his side. "It's so good to have you back, Kel." He gave her a lengthy embrace, and then before releasing her, he kissed her cheek.

Time briefly stood still as Kelli's heart skipped a beat, and then it began to race out of control.

Chapter 5

After Kelli had returned home that night and slipped into bed, she found that she couldn't go to sleep. Instead her mind kept replaying the evening with Jace, and she had felt so at ease with him while they were at the restaurant talking about their families, their educations, and their dreams. She had even shared with him the fact that she had gone out on a limb and bought an arabechia farm. She knew it was a risk, but she was financially stable enough to chance it. However, if it didn't pay off she would probably need to be looking for work in a couple more years. She realized and accepted this fact and was at ease to follow her dreams at this point in her life. If those dreams meant quitting her boring but financially sound job, then so be it. Life was just too short to spend it doing something which brought no satisfaction. Kelli had known too many people who had planned to someday follow their dream or take a risk, but it never came to fruition for them. Life—or fate—so often had other plans for them.

The only point all evening when Kelli had felt ill at ease was when Jace had embraced her and kissed her cheek. She had immediately felt such a strange tingle throughout her body, and her heart had begun beating wildly. There was something about Jace that created electricity in her body whenever he touched her. He hadn't appeared to have been affected by the quick kiss, so Kelli had tried to act like it was nothing, either. However, her heart rate certainly didn't return to normal for a long while afterward.

Kelli didn't hear from Jace for most of the following week. She threw herself into work at the house and was satisfied with the way it all was coming together. The bathroom tile which she had selected had come in, and she had scheduled a time for the workers to begin installing it the following week.

Meanwhile, Mr. Mills had begun pulling out all the existing kitchen appliances and replacing sheetrock in the areas that needed it. Kelli had decided not to replace the kitchen cabinets since they were made of solid wood. They would need to be sanded and primed, but with the addition of new paint and hardware, they would look completely new. The old flooring had been finally pulled up throughout the house, and where there were not hardwood floors, she would choose new carpeting.

Mrs. Tanner had visited twice during the week, bringing coffee and warm banana muffins one morning and tea and ham sandwiches for lunch another day. She was so happy to have the house being fixed up again, but even more so to have Kelli back as her neighbor.

"I just don't think that you are eating enough," she had said with a worried expression to Kelli one day. "You look so thin, so I brought over some sandwiches. Now, take a break and be sure to eat a couple."

Kelli thanked her and hugged her tightly as she bit into a sandwich, realizing that she really was hungry but just hadn't taken the time to notice. It was nice to have Mrs. Tanner looking out for her and was like living next door to her beloved grandmother.

Late afternoon on Thursday, Jace strolled into the bedroom where Kelli was prying a loose board off the closet wall.

"Hi," he said, as Kelli whirled around in his direction. "I didn't want to scare you. Guess you couldn't hear me knocking on the back door."

"Sorry, come on in. It's just one big construction zone around here, anyway," Kelli said, as she walked over to where he stood. "What do you think of the house? Can you tell there's been any improvement since the last time you saw it?"

"Definitely," Jace said with an approving look.

Kelli briefly showed him the bathroom and kitchen areas and explained what was being done next in the remodeling process. She stopped in mid-sentence when she finally realized he was obviously either going or coming from work since he was dressed in slacks and a dress shirt.

"Am I keeping you?" she asked him. "I got so absorbed in showing you around that I didn't ask if you had time to look."

"I've got about an hour before I return to the hospital for my evening rounds. It's been such a hectic week, and I'm sorry that I haven't talked with you since our dinner. When I get home at night this place is dark, and you've already gone to your apartment."

He put his hands in his pockets. "I was wondering if you'd like to go with me to a barbeque Saturday evening at a neighbor's house. He lives down the street and is an astronomy professor at the local university. If the sky is clear he always gives a fascinating look at the night sky, and I thought it would be a nice chance for you to meet some of your new neighbors."

"That sounds terrific," Kelli said, realizing that she was anxious to meet the people who would soon be her neighbors. "What can I bring?"

"You just bring yourself, and I'll furnish some drinks as our contribution." He paused a moment before adding, "On second thought, bring your bathing suit."

Kelli blinked, looking somewhat confused. "Is it a pool party at this time of year?" she asked.

"No, but I have a hot tub, and if the stars are out that evening we can go back to my place and soak in the tub while we attempt to locate the constellations that I'm sure we will learn about."

Kelli felt a slight hesitation come over her, but brushed it quickly aside. After all, they were once best buddies. Why should she feel the slightest bit uncomfortable sharing a hot tub with him now?

"What time do I need to meet you there?"

"I'll pick you up at your place at 7:00."

He complimented her again on the progress that she and Mr. Mills were making with the house, warned her not to work too hard, and then left to head back to the hospital.

Kelli went into the living room and sat down on the bare floor, leaning her head against the wall and surveying the entire room. It sure was a mess, she thought as she looked around. There was scuffed flooring, chipped paint on the walls, and cobwebs everywhere. She decided that her next step would be to wipe down the walls and ceiling in here and apply fresh paint. All this room really needed was paint and for the hardwood floor to be restored.

As she sat there, she found herself again reminiscing about living here as a child. She could visualize her family's annual Christmas tree, freshly-cut and covered in silver tinsel, standing in the far corner. She remembered her parents' beige sofa sitting against the wall to her right. A pile of zebra pillows, which her mom had sewed, had once been stacked neatly in the area beside where Kelli sat. The living room now encompassed her bedroom, since the wall dividing the two rooms had been removed years earlier. Kelli realized that she was sitting near where her bed had been as a girl. As she looked out the windows, she vividly remembered this very view as she had lain in bed at night.

It was a surreal experience to return here as an adult. The house had seemed so much larger in her memories. In reality, it was just a small bungalow, but nonetheless, it was a bungalow filled with precious family memories. As she continued to reflect on all that had happened within these walls as she was growing up, she shivered as she remembered the apparition of the young girl that she frequently had seen here. It had occurred over there, she thought to herself, as she looked toward the small hallway connecting the kitchen to the living room.

She arose and walked over to the spot, as if half-expecting the apparition to instantly appear. Would she see her again, now that she was a grown woman? Or was the ghost's appearance only shared with those who were closer to her own age? Kelli had not much considered the very real possibility of seeing her again once she began spending nights in this house.

She spent Friday and Saturday working on the living room, as she had decided. She had chosen a taupe paint color, and by noon Saturday she had applied a coat of primer and two coats of paint to the walls. It looked like an entirely different room, she thought, as she hammered the lid back on the paint can.

By late afternoon she had returned home and successfully scrubbed most of the paint off her skin, although she couldn't get it entirely out of her hair. She was not a very neat painter she realized with a smile, since she wore almost as much paint on herself as she had applied to the walls. However, she did her best to clean up enough to meet the neighbors tonight. She decided to wear blue jeans and a long-sleeved navy blouse with ruffles cascading down the front. The spring days were mild and beautiful in Arkansas, but the evenings could become cool quickly once the sun set.

Kelli heard Jace drive up at 7:00, punctual as usual, she thought, as she looked out of the window. She walked to the door and greeted him warmly. He was wearing jeans and a dark polo shirt and this combination made him look ruggedly handsome in a chic way. He stepped inside the door and remarked how pretty she looked.

"Just don't look too closely at my hair," Kelli told him, "or you'll see paint still in it. I washed it twice, but it won't all come out."

"At least it's close to the color of your hair," Jace told her. "It could have been green or red paint."

"Wouldn't that have been great?" extolled Kelli, her voice dripping with sarcasm. "Meeting new neighbors for the first time with hair looking like that of a punk rocker's."

Jace laughed at this idea as they walked to his car. He opened her door for her and then walked around to the other side to get in. As he lowered his tall frame into the seat, he turned to ask her if she had remembered her bathing suit.

"It's packed in my bag," said Kelli. "So, you've added a hot tub to your parents' place?"

"It's nothing, really. Just a small one out back on the patio. It is a wonderful way for me to unwind each night after being on my feet most of the day. Very therapeutic." He glanced left and then right as he pulled out onto the street. "You are welcome to use it each evening after working on the house all day. It does wonders for sore muscles."

"I can visualize you coming home from a long day at work and finding me sitting in your hot tub," said Kelli with a sneer.

"So can I," deadpanned Jace. "And I like the image that I visualize."

They chatted easily the short drive back to the neighborhood and Jace pulled into the driveway of a house three doors down from Kelli's own. He explained that the guy who lived there, Matt, is single, an astronomy professor, and that he gives fabulous star parties throughout the year, the best one being in December during the Geminids meteor shower. Guests bring blankets to wrap up in as they sit on his patio and watch falling stars. Last year he held the party on an incredibly clear, but cold, night. Meteors were falling at a rate of several every half hour, and it was definitely worth putting up with the cold for.

When they arrived at Matt's house several cars were already there. They walked to the back yard, and Kelli was impressed by the sight of three large telescopes set up around the area. There was smoke coming from a large grill creating a tantalizing aroma, and nearby a table bearing a brightly-colored cloth was brimming with food. Music was playing on speakers strategically placed around the patio, and guests were mingling and laughing as Jace led Kelli onto the patio.

Matt approached them and Jace encircled Kelli's waist with his arm.

"Matt, this is Kelli Evans, the newest member of our neighborhood."

Matt extended his hand to Kelli. "The newest 'returning' member, I hear. It's so nice to finally meet you, Kelli. I've heard so much about you and all the childhood shenanigans that you and Jace pulled. It must be quite an experience to move back into the home that you lived in as a girl. I'm sure there are memories everywhere you turn."

"Yes, there are," Kelli answered, shaking his hand. "Currently, I'm in the middle of having the entire place renovated. I'm afraid that it has turned into quite an eyesore over the past several years, as I'm sure you've noticed."

"I'll be the first to admit that I was thrilled to learn you were buying the place and fixing it up. It will definitely improve the neighborhood and add value to all of our homes, as well."

Matt then changed the subject. "I understand that you worked for an investment firm up North. Will you be involved with that again, here, after you get settled?"

"I doubt it, but I can't say what doors will eventually open up for me here. Basically, I just missed seeing green grass and pastures, mountains and blue skies. It's heaven here in Arkansas; don't let anyone ever convince you that the grass is greener on the other side of the fence."

Matt nodded in agreement. "I was born and raised in Chicago. When I got the job at the university here, I thought I would be moving to where only rednecks and hillbillies lived. Was I ever mistaken! I'm now trying to persuade my parents and siblings to move down here."

"I understand your star parties are a smashing success," Kelli said. "When did you become interested in astronomy?"

"When I was a young boy," Matt replied. "I got my first telescope for Christmas when I was eight and that began my fascination with stars, constellations and meteors. I've been fortunate to participate in some meteorite digs in Australia and Scotland. We found small fragments, nothing big, but the hope of finding the big one exists each time you begin a hunt. Most of the time I share my fascination with students at the university and give tours to area grade schools, as well."

They continued chatting for a while longer and then Matt insisted they help themselves to the drinks. A little while later he introduced them to more people while they were walking around, sipping their drinks. Most of the people lived in the neighborhood, and Jace knew everyone there. They were all happy to meet the woman whom they had heard about and were glad that she was renovating the deteriorated house down the road. Kelli tried to remember names and learn who lived in which house. In time, she was sure it would all click. Everyone seemed very friendly, and there were many families present. It was interesting to place these people in houses that she had known of other families living in when she was a child. The house at the end of the street used to be inhabited by a family of five; now, a young couple with a baby called that place home. It was nice to think that the neighborhood was still thriving.

As the evening progressed, food and drinks were served, laughter was shared, and engaging conversation was prevalent. When it was dark, everyone gathered around the telescopes and Matt gave a short little spiel on the planets they would be looking at tonight. Of course, he also pointed out many constellations and told a brief history of each one, how it got its name, what the early settlers believed they meant, and so on. Kelli was extremely fascinated by it all since she didn't know that much about astronomy to begin with. As she looked through a telescope at one point, she was actually able to see Saturn's ring. All the craters and dips of the moon's surface were also magnified through the telescopes, as well as binoculars that guests had brought.

By the end of the evening Kelli was glad that Jace had invited her to the party where she had met so many of her new neighbors. Now, when she saw them outside in their yards she would at least know their names and a little about each one. One of the young wives, Morgan, even suggested that they have lunch together soon. Kelli sensed that they had a lot in common and welcomed the chance at making a new friend.

When Jace and Kelli said their goodbyes, the party was winding down, and most people were also leaving. They drove down the road to Jace's house where he led her inside and pointed to the hall bathroom for her to change into her bathing suit. A few moments later Kelli emerged and walked into the kitchen wearing a red halter-style suit with gold banding around the middle and she had loosely pinned her hair up on top of her head to keep it out of the water. Jace was standing against the counter, already wearing his swim trunks, and did a double-take at her as she joined him.

He let out a low whistle. "You look stunning, Kel."

She brushed it off and tried not to look at his long, muscular legs. When had he grown so tall?

They went out the back door and followed a sidewalk to the small patio behind the house. Jace opened the cover of the hot tub and held her hand as she climbed in. The air outside was cool and crisp which made the frothy, hot water feel heavenly as she scooted down the bench seat. Jace climbed in and sat beside her. Wisps of steam were rising into the cool night air, and the sky overhead was filled with so many stars it appeared as if a huge city of twinkling lights was spread above them. They were silent for a few moments, enjoying the quietness, the beauty of the stars, and the comfort of each other's presence.

Jace finally broke the silence when he pointed to a northern constellation and told her it was named "Berenice's Hair."

"Want to know why it's named that?" he asked, and when she nodded, he continued.

"It's a romantic tale about an Egyptian queen who cut off her golden locks to give to the goddess of love in exchange for keeping her husband safe at war. The goddess was so happy with the hair that she took it up to heaven and turned it into a cluster of stars."

"That's a lovely story," Kelli said, while gazing at the shimmering cluster of stars.

"Yes, it is. Many of the constellations have names and meanings that are steeped in mythology."

"Is astronomy a hobby of yours?" she asked.

"No, not really," answered Jace, sheepishly. "I've just hung out with Matt enough for a little bit of his knowledge to rub off on me. As you saw tonight, his parties are fun, but guests always learn a little about the night sky, too."

He turned to look at Kelli. "What about you? Do you believe in Greek mythology, or witches, warlocks, vampires and all that stuff?"

"Greek mythology is interesting. I also like a good vampire movie, but the rest I don't believe in." She sunk down a little deeper in the warm, bubbling water. "However, there is something . . ." she hesitated. "Well, never mind. Forget it."

"Forget what? You can't just leave me hanging like that," prodded Jace. "Come on, tell me," he urged, poking her foot with his big toe.

"Okay. When I lived here as a little girl, I often would see the form of a young girl walking out of the kitchen toward me," she hesitated again, suddenly feeling immensely silly for even bringing the subject up. "Though I never could make out her face, she had brown, shoulder-length hair, and wore a navy dress. Oh, and she always had either a doll—-or a baby—-on her hip. I would only see her late at night and, oddly, it never scared me." She pursed her lips and added, "The way it would now."

"I vaguely remember that sometimes when we were playing, you commented on having seen 'the little girl' again. I never thought anything of it back then, just that you were probably referring to an imaginary friend. So, what are you saying now . . . that you think you were seeing the ghost of a young girl?"

"That's exactly what I think. Do you remember that gravesite over on the edge of the woods that we sometimes would ride our bikes to see?"

"You mean that lone, worn granite tombstone sticking out of the brush that used to creep us out? The one that we neighborhood kids would dare each other to walk over and touch?" He could make out Kelli's eyes watching him intently in the shadowy darkness. "Yeah, I remember it."

Kelli sighed and then leaned her head back on the ridge of the hot tub to gaze up at the prickling of stars again, as if searching for the right words before continuing. "When I was in my late teens one day, I was remembering both the ghostly apparition and the tombstone, and I put two and two together. Do you remember what we were all told about that grave when we were kids?"

"Only that it belonged to a girl who died at a young age." Jace put his fingers on his forehead as if to help him think deeper. "I recall hearing that it was the grave of the original farm owner's daughter—or something to that effect."

"That's what I was always told, also. Curiously, the Shroeder family who once owned much of this land in the neighborhood originally lived in my family's home."

A cold shiver suddenly ran up Jace's spine, despite sitting in the steamy water. This made a little too much sense and all at once seemed a little too real. He turned to Kelli, a worried tone in his voice. "You said you were never scared as a child when you saw this apparition. Did you ever feel threatened or stalked?"

"No, no, nothing ever like that. It was almost as if the little girl wanted to play or something," Kelli tried to explain. "She always appeared friendly."

"At least she was not a menacing ghost," Jace said. "Listen to me! I can't believe I'm even talking about ghosts. I never believed in that stuff before, and certainly never knew anyone who experienced something like this."

He pulled himself out of the water and sat on the edge of the hot tub. "Looks like we've got our own little mystery to solve, Kel."

Chapter 6

J ace had driven Kelli home and promised to call her soon. Before he'd left, he had thanked her for trusting him enough to share the ghost experience with him and was intrigued enough to want to investigate it further. As Kelli had undressed for bed, she felt a little embarrassed for spilling the story to Jace. She didn't know why she felt the need to tell him her childhood experience with a ghost, she thought, with a roll of her eyes. But he was so darned easy to talk to, and it was him who had even brought up the subject in the first place. He was talking about mythology and stars, and then one thing led to another, and before she knew it she was blabbing about her ghost experiences. This probably sealed the deal for him in thinking she was a crazy woman, first by quitting a fabulous job and moving back to her rundown childhood home and then by talking about a ghost that had lived in that same house. Kelli was sure that Jace had thought she'd lost her mind.

The next afternoon Jace walked across the street to Kelli's house. It was a Sunday, and he had already visited his patients at the hospital. He was on call, but no emergencies had been called in, as of yet.

Kelli was sanding the kitchen cabinets when she heard a knock on the back door. She peeped out the window and saw Jace standing there and motioned for him to come in.

"Hi," she said, as she looked up at him from beneath her lashes, a tinge of embarrassment coloring her cheeks. "Did you dream about ghosts last night?"

"No, but I've done a lot of thinking about what you told me." He turned around slowly, looking at his surroundings. "Didn't you say the

47

sightings occurred here in the kitchen?" He gestured around. "Show me where."

Kelli put her sandpaper down and walked over to the small hallway off the entrance to the kitchen. "She would be walking out of the kitchen, where you are standing, coming toward this hallway." She pointed out the path with her hand. "I would pause here and look in at her on the way down the corridor. She would keep walking slowly toward me, and she was always carrying either a doll or a baby. I remember her wearing a navy dress and having shoulder-length brown hair, but her face was not defined. It always just appeared to be the shape of a face, sort of fuzzy and hazy."

Jace let out a long breath. "Gee, if that had happened to me as a kid, I'd have been terrified."

"The funny thing is, I was never scared of her and got to where I actually expected to see her. It became our ritual. I guess she sensed that I was a little girl, like herself, and she just wanted to be friends. I've read that young children are often more susceptible to ghost experiences than adults are because their minds are open." She shrugged. "I guess that's what was happening here."

"Your brother never saw her, correct?"

"If he did, he never admitted it. But, I used to tell him that I had seen her the previous night, and he would just listen and nod, with his eyes big and round. I look back now and realize he probably thought his sister had a great imagination."

Jace walked over to where Kelli stood and put his hand on her shoulder. "Do you have any hesitancy about perhaps having another sighting of her once you move back into this house? Any fears or concerns?"

"I must admit that the possibility of her appearing to me again has crossed my mind. Will she know that I'm the same little girl who used to

48

live here? Is she still even haunting this house? I mean, geez, I don't know the thought processes or intellectual capacities of ghosts."

Jace gave her a reassuring hug as Kelli continued. "All I know is that I love this little house and everything it represents to me of my past—so many happy memories, holiday gatherings, birthday parties, laughter. Even as an adult this house showed up in many of my dreams, and I continue to feel such a connection to it. I won't let this one, small drawback run me off."

"That's my girl, tough as nails. You know, you were always such a tomboy and nothing intimidated you. I'm glad to see that you haven't changed in that respect."

Kelli looked up into Jace's eyes and saw the tenderness there. His arm was still around her, and he placed his other arm around her waist and drew her to him. They stood there, very still, staring into each other's eyes, as if daring the other to admit that a fire was unmistakably simmering somewhere under the surface between them. The friendship they shared as a little boy and girl was so sweet and innocent. Now, what was once childish innocence was being replaced by something entirely different, and it was pulling them together like magnets.

Jace's face grew serious as he searched her face, from her questioning eyes, down to her full lips, then back to those liquid green eyes. Kelli felt her heart beating so furiously that she was sure Jace could feel it against his chest. He slowly lowered his face until his lips tasted hers ever so softly, tentatively, lovingly.

He pulled away after one long, glorious moment, never taking his eyes from hers. She could see the confusion that clouded them. "I'm sorry, Kel, I don't know what came over me."

Kelli cleared her throat and took a step back. "Don't be. I certainly didn't resist."

She could still feel his warm lips on hers, and her heart had yet to find its normal rhythm. She walked him to the door, said goodbye and then closed the door behind her, leaning back against it with her arms crossed. She ran her fingers through her hair in agitation. What was wrong with her? Jace had been her closest friend as a child, someone she'd known and trusted as well as her own brother. He was like a member of her family. Any sort of romantic feelings between the two of them would most certainly dissolve their deep, abiding friendship. She didn't want that, and she was sure that Jace didn't either. True, any red-blooded woman would naturally be attracted to Jace. After all, he was a tall, lean, handsome man with gorgeous eyes, and charm that seemed to drip from his pores. Throw into the mix the fact that he is a well-respected cardiologist and women everywhere must swoon at his feet. Nonetheless, Kelli firmly understood that she must ignore any feelings of attraction to him if she truly valued their friendship and wanted it to last.

* * * * * *

Much work was accomplished over the following week with Mr. Mills arriving early each day and staying late. His pay was based on the project itself, rather than an hourly wage, but he had another job after this one and was anxious to get as much done as quickly as possible. He was meticulous in his work, and Kelli was impressed by his skill. He was also a genuinely nice older man, and Kelli was glad that she had chosen him for the job. She would certainly recommend him to others if her advice was ever sought.

After Kelli had sanded and primed the cabinets, he showed her a technique using stain and paint that would give the cabinets an Old World charm, which was the look that she was after. He also helped her decide on a paint technique that she was anxious to try on the kitchen walls that would impart a flavor reminiscent of Tuscany to the room. Add a wrought iron chandelier over a glass and iron table, a few tall plants in terra cotta pots and the room would be exactly like Kelli had imagined.

50

For years she had collected pictures in magazines of rooms and styles that she adored and had compiled a thick folder of ideas. It was now time to pull these ideas out and put them to use. Kelli had an innate sense of style and knew the look she was after. She could see a room in disrepair and imagine how it would look after it was remodeled. Her friends had told her this was a gift, and that she should become an interior decorator, but Kelli was happy to use the ideas on her own home for now.

One afternoon a delivery truck pulled up to Jace's house, and upon the driver finding no one there, he saw Kelli outdoors, pulled his truck over to the side of the street, and walked over to her yard. He had a delivery for one of the builders and needed someone to sign for it, so he asked her if she would be willing. She agreed, and he handed her the box.

That evening Kelli had stayed late to paint the kitchen walls, and it was nearly nine o'clock when she got ready to leave and remembered the box that had been left for Jace. She drove over on her way home, and when she saw lights on in the house she started to jump out, but noticed another car there. She hesitated for a brief moment, but then decided to go ahead and rid herself of the responsibility of delivering it.

She walked to his back door, tired and dirty, aware of how she must appear with paint splattered all over her clothes and probably all over her face and hair, too. Oh, well, she thought, she wasn't trying to impress him. This would be the first time that they had spoken since *the kiss.* She knocked on the door and when Jace swung it open she looked over his shoulder and saw a stunning brunette with legs to her neck sitting on the couch in the living room. The brunette looked questioningly at Kelli and smiled slowly, as Jace stood there holding the door open, shifting from one foot to the other and looking as if he would rather be anywhere else in the world at this moment.

"Sorry to bother you, but I have a package for you." She hated the iciness that her voice held. "A delivery truck driver left this for your builder this afternoon. No one was at the jobsite, and when he saw me across the road he asked if I would sign for it." She handed Jace the package and turned to leave.

"Kelli, wait! I mean . . . thanks," he said, as he looked over his shoulder at the brunette waiting for him. He stepped outside and closed the door behind him, his hand still on the doorknob as he spoke. "Look, this isn't what it appears," he began.

Kelli held up her hand and stopped him before he could continue. "You certainly don't owe me any explanation," she said rather too brusquely. "We're simply two old friends from the past. I don't care who you entertain in your own house." She sounded like she was trying to convince herself. "Look, you've got company waiting and I'm bushed, not to mention in bad need of a hot bath. See you around." She turned on her heel and walked quickly back to her car.

"Kelli!" Jace called after her, but she had already climbed in her car and closed the door. She drove home feeling upset with herself for even having any type of reaction at all to seeing a woman sitting in Jace's house. She remembered how he had told her that he wasn't currently involved with anyone, that he didn't have time for relationships, but how could she honestly believe that a handsome, eligible bachelor, who also happened to be a doctor, didn't entertain women? They were probably knocking on his door every chance they got.

Kelli pulled into the parking lot of her apartment complex hungry, exhausted, and disillusioned, trying to convince herself that she could not care any less about seeing a woman on Jace's couch.

The next day Kelli threw herself into her work at an even more intense pace than she previously had. In fact, she had decided that it just might be time to spend the night for the first time in her new house. After all, the living room and bedroom were finished, except for the hardwood floor being restored, and that was scheduled to be done next week. The kitchen appliances were ordered and would likewise be arriving the next week. The walls were painted, the kitchen cabinets were refinished, and a new terra cotta tile floor would be installed in there soon. The extra guest bedroom, a new half bath, and the loft area were all that remained to be finished. That work could be performed even if Kelli were living in the house. Nonetheless, she felt it would be fun to camp out there that night.

Late in the afternoon, Jace walked over, and found Kelli sweeping the floor in the living room. "Hey," he said cautiously as he stepped closer to her. "I want to explain about last night."

Kelli held up her hand in protest, cutting him off before he could continue. "Look, it's none of my business who was in your house or what you were doing." She began sweeping with more speed and briskness than was necessary. "You and I are both free to date whoever we want, whenever we want. It's no big deal." She shrugged as if it helped make her point. "Besides, we're old friends, nothing more."

With that being said, Jace stepped closer still. "Kelli, I may be nothing more than an old friend to you, but you are somebody special to me. I find you attractive and intelligent and interesting to be around." His penetrating eyes reminded her of the color of a mourning dove. "Last night Stella came over uninvited. She's a nurse in the intensive care unit at the hospital, and when I first moved back to town, I took her to dinner a couple of times. She finds excuses to drop by my house from time to time unannounced."

"She's drop-dead gorgeous," Kelli interrupted. "Most guys would never find it an inopportune time for someone like her to drop by unannounced."

"She's a beautiful girl, I'll agree," Jace said. "But, we have nothing in common with each other except that we both understand the medical field. At the end of the day, I'd rather not sit and discuss medical conditions with a date." His eyes had changed from pleading to affirming. "Is that a deal?"

Kelli's sweeping came to a halt, and she leaned on the broom handle. "Deal. You won't have to worry about me ever sitting around and discussing the intricate workings of a heart with you," she tartly replied.

Jace nodded at the broom. "What are you doing in here anyway? Are they coming to finish the floor tomorrow?" he asked, looking around the room.

"Not until next week. But, I thought it might be kind of fun to spend my first night here tonight."

"Tonight? Where are you going to sleep without any furniture?" asked Jace.

"I thought I'd just make a pallet on the floor here and camp out." When she saw Jace's expression she added, "It will be fun!"

"How about I bring my truck, and we at least go to your apartment and get your couch or bed or something for you to sleep on?"

"Oh, no, I don't want you to go to any trouble. I'd planned on making a simple pallet of blankets to sleep on."

"Come on, kid," he said, pulling her toward the back door. "Do it for me. You think I'll be able to sleep tonight knowing you are over here sleeping on a cold, hard floor?" He stuck his bottom lip out in mock reproach. "Besides, it's not even been refinished and waxed, yet."

"As if that would matter," laughed Kelli, allowing him to pull her by the arm out the door, across the back yard, and toward his house.

They drove in Jace's truck to her apartment, and once there Kelli decided to take a small twin bed that she was going to use in the guest room. "You know, Jace," she said, as he lowered the tailgate of his truck so that they could load the bedframe first, "this is totally unnecessary. I was going to camp out in the floor without any bed at all and be perfectly happy about it."

54

"So, you are the 'roughing it' kind of gal, huh? No luxury hotels for you?"

"I didn't say that," she clarified, while helping shove the mattress in next.

Jace shut the tailgate and suggested that she look around to see what else she would need to pack for the night. "Don't forget to pack something for breakfast," he suggested. "As for dinner tonight, I was wondering if you'd mind stopping by Cal's Diner with me. They have terrific cheeseburgers and shakes."

"Jace, look at me!" She swept her hand down the front of her sweatshirt as if to emphasize the grunge. "I don't want to go out like this!"

"How do you plan to shower or bathe tonight?" he asked her with his arms crossed. "The knobs and faucets in your bathroom are not even installed, yet."

Kelli looked slightly embarrassed at having forgotten this simple fact. "I had planned on driving over here tonight to clean up when I came for my blankets and pillows. That is, until you totally caught me off guard and insisted on dragging me over here to load up a bed." She didn't want to admit that his presence frazzled her nerves and left her mind in a haze.

A smile tugged at the corners of Jace's mouth and he turned toward her front door. "I'll just go in and make myself comfortable in your living room while you shower. I suppose you've got a cold drink I can have while waiting?"

She rolled her eyes at him and nodded while she walked back into her house, holding the door open behind her for Jace. It didn't take her long to shower and dress, and as promised, she found a coke in the refrigerator for Jace as he waited for her while watching television. She put on a pair of blue jeans and a long-sleeved blouse and packed a few essentials, along with her gown, into a night bag. "All set," she said as she walked into the living room.

Jace let out a low whistle. "You sure clean up well, Kelli," he said admiringly.

"It's amazing what a bar of soap and some water can do, isn't it?" Kelli retorted.

On the drive to Kelli's house, they stopped at Cal's Diner, as Jace had requested. It was a lively establishment, with a 50's decor inside and flashing neon lights outside. Tables were covered in striped tablecloths, a jukebox sat in the corner, and booths lined three walls. The room's focal point was the rather imposing, front half of a pink, 1954 Cadillac mounted on the back mirrored wall. Waiters and waitresses were dressed in vintage 50's attire, and the place was bustling with customers. Despite the kinetic energy the room exuded, Jace and Kelli had a leisurely and extremely enjoyable meal while sitting in a back corner booth.

"So, are you a little nervous about possibly seeing her tonight?" Jace asked, in between bites of his juicy cheeseburger.

A blank look registered on Kelli's face a moment before she realized who he was talking about. She put her burger back down in the paper-lined basket. "I haven't thought too much lately about it, but it's a definite possibility with my staying in the house again. This may sound weird, but I wonder if she will recognize me? After all, it's been over 20 years. Can she sense that I'm the same Kelli she appeared to when I was a child? I don't know. Plus, the house has been lived in by a few different families since my family left and some structural changes have been made to it."

"Are you saying that maybe the sound of hammers and saws ran her off? Or that the other people who lived in the house had no young daughter with whom she could interact?"

Kelli shrugged. "I don't know what to think. I don't know much about the lifestyles and personalities of ghosts." She gave a meek smile.

56

"Well, my dear, if anyone can rouse her again, it will be you."

They finished their meal and walked outside to get in Jace's truck. "Looks like we'd better hurry and get this bed unloaded," said Jace, looking up at the sky. "Those look like some menacing clouds moving in."

They had both been so busy that day that they had not listened to the local weather. They were just entering their neighborhood, and Jace backed his truck into Kelli's driveway to help ease their unloading. They carried the twin bed in through the front door, and it was quickly set up in the bedroom. It could easily be moved when the floor refinishers came to work. Kelli thanked Jace for all his help and reluctantly admitted that it would indeed be more comfortable to sleep on a mattress rather than a pallet on the floor.

"Looks like there could be a bad storm tonight," Jace said, as he walked to the front door. "Make sure everything is latched down, and call me if you need something."

Kelli assured him that she would, her cell phone was tucked in her purse, and thanked him again for all his help and for dinner. After he left she sat down on the little bed and planned where she would place her bedroom furniture in this room. Although she had worked long hours on this house, she had not actually had the privilege to sit inside, think and plan its interior. After a while she walked throughout the rooms, marveling at the beautiful transformation of much of it, noting what projects still laid ahead. She was anxious to finish the actual work so that she could get down to the fun of decorating and placing furniture within the rooms. She visualized how the finished kitchen would look and how the living room would appear and made another mental note to go shopping for drapes soon.

It was so good to be back, she thought. She checked the locks on all the doors and made sure the windows were securely shut. As she looked out the kitchen window she saw thick, black, angry clouds gathering from the west. No doubt a bad storm would probably be imminent during the night. Since she had no television or radio in the house yet, she took out the thick novel which she had brought along and settled down for a cozy, first night back in her childhood home. She read for a couple hours before falling asleep while still holding the book, and since there was not a lamp yet in the house, the overhead bedroom light was on.

It was either the light flickering off and on or the loud clap of thunder outside her window that woke her from a deep sleep. The lights flickered off and on a couple more times, and then totally went out.

Great, thought Kelli. She didn't even have candles in the house, yet. She did have a flashlight outside in her car, but she was unwilling to step out to retrieve it when she looked outside. Heavy sheets of rain were coming down furiously and lightning bolts were slashing the sky, followed by horrendous booms of thunder. When the next bolt of lightning lit up the neighborhood like daylight, Kelli saw the trees between her house and Mrs. Tanner's bending almost completely over.   The loose window shutters, which still needed to be repainted and securely bolted, were clanging against the house. Mingled with all the noise was a different thudding sound—almost a banging—and it was difficult to make out what it was because everything sounded so loud and confusing. As she felt her way around the dark house, looking out the windows, she heard the thudding again, but this time accompanied by something that sounded like yelling. She made her way to the back door and heard it again, this time more clearly.

Chapter 7

elli, open up! It's me, Jace! Open up!"

Kelli's fingers groped along the doorframe, feeling for the lock, and after finding it, she twisted the knob, swinging the door open at the exact same moment that Jace was pushing on it from the other side. He came barreling through the door, his six-foot, four frame covered in a dripping rain slicker. He didn't have time to find his galoshes, but on the way out of his house had just grabbed his sneakers, which were now completely soaked. He plowed into her, sending her spiraling backward until she hit the wall.

"What in the . . . ?" began Kelli, but she didn't have time to finish her question because he grabbed her hand and in one fluid moment had her up on her feet again, shoving her toward the bathroom, which was difficult to do in the pitch blackness of the room.

"Quick," he commanded, as he felt his way around the bathroom until his fingers found the edge of the shower entry. "In here! Now! Lie down!" He quickly pushed her to the floor on her belly and then landed on top of her, covering her body with his own in protection. Outside, lightning bolts were striking all about and the wind was howling and shrieking fiercely around the house, followed by deafening booms of thunder. Suddenly, it was eerily quiet, as if Mother Nature had pushed some sort of button and ceased the storm.

"Jace, what is going on? Why did you . . . ?"

"Tornado," he interrupted in a curt voice. "One was spotted a couple miles away, not on the ground but capable of spinning down at any moment." He hesitated before continuing. "We are directly in its path. I tried calling you, but I guess cell service is down."

"Jace!" Kelli said in a panic, trying to scramble out from under him and stand up. "Mrs. Tanner! We've got to warn her or at least check on her!" Jace's grip on her arm tightened so that she couldn't escape.

"Hold on," he said, trying to keep her down. "She's safe at her daughter's house. She called me when she saw what was happening since she knows I always check on her during bad weather."

Mrs. Tanner had always been like a grandmother to them, and Kelli found that she was both relieved and touched that he still checked on her and treated her as such.

Lying in the close confines of the shower, Kelli was keenly aware of Jace's long, muscular body pressed on top of hers. She tried to steady her own breathing, not completely sure if her thudding heart was exclusively due to her fear of a pending tornado or the fact that Jace was lying on top of her. His soaking rain slicker had saturated her gown, and now she was soaked, as well. The tornado sirens were blaring in the distance, but as they laid still and listened, there was no sound that resembled that of a roaring freight train, the common description of a tornado as it ripped through an area.

After what seemed like an hour, but was in reality only a few minutes, Jace muttered, "I'm going to get up and check outside, see what's going on. You stay here," he ordered.

She struggled to get up and follow him despite what he just said, but he gently, yet firmly, pushed her back down. "Please, Kelli, it's not safe, yet. Let me check things out, and I'll be back."

She relented and lay back down against the cold tile listening as his wet sneakers noisily squished through the bathroom door and into the kitchen. She heard him pause at the window and figured he must be trying to see out into the blackness. Since the power had been knocked out, the neighborhood sat in complete darkness. She heard him walk to the back door, open it, and step outside. She waited for what felt like an eternity before she heard the door reopen and his footsteps noisily returning to the shower where she was still waiting.

"It appears that we're out of danger. It's just raining lightly out there, and I suspect the wall cloud is well past now. It was a close call, though."

Kelli stood up and made her way out of the bathroom with Jace. She was shivering slightly in her wet gown and was sure that Jace was probably cold and very uncomfortable too, since he was totally drenched. "Thanks for making sure I was safe, Jace. I had no idea that a tornado was in the area. I guess what woke me were either the lights blinking or the loud thunder. I'm just glad that the house didn't blow away."

"That would have been lousy. You buy your childhood house and before you get it remodeled and ready to move into, it blows away in a tornado."

"I would take that as a sign that it was not meant to be for me to move back," Kelli said, crossing her arms in front of her chest. "But, it appears that I've made the right decision, at least for now."

Jace stepped closer to her. "Do you always believe in signs, Kelli?" He couldn't see her face, so he reached out and wrapped his arms around her shoulders, pulling her close against his broad shoulders. She felt so small and vulnerable in her damp gown and it tugged at his heart.

"I do," she answered. "Don't you?"

"Maybe." His voice sounded deep and throaty as he cupped her chin with his hand. Slowly, he lowered his face to hers in the darkness, knowing exactly where her mouth awaited. He brushed his lips softly against hers, testing and teasing, and then deepened the kiss, causing Kelli's head to spin in foolish pleasure. She reached up, wrapped her arms around his neck and eagerly returned the kiss, totally lost in the moment, an eager accomplice in this surprising and spontaneous act. Her heart was beating crazily, and she knew Jace could probably feel it, too, through the thin, damp material of her gown.

He pulled back slightly, but kept his arms wrapped around her. "So, tell me Kel. Do you take that as a good sign, too?"

"Maybe," she replied, echoing his earlier answer, her mind still reeling from the kiss.

"I hope so. I think we are good together, always were. We have a history together, it doesn't matter that we were young; what matters is that you know me for who I am, who I was, what I believe in. That hasn't changed. The only thing that has changed is the passage of time."

He backed up and reached for the doorknob. "Now, do you think you will be able to get some more sleep before morning?"

"I'll try. What about you? Do you have to be at the hospital early?"

"Yes, but I doubt that I'll be able to go back to sleep now, anyway. I'll give you a call later," he said softly and then stepped forward to give her a chaste kiss on her cheek.

"Jace?" Kelli softly asked.

"Yes?"

"Thank you." She could feel the heat rising in her cheeks and was thankful for the darkness. "I mean . . . for coming to check on me."

She couldn't see that his eyes were twinkling and a smile was on his lips.

"My pleasure." He closed the door behind him and took off on foot back to his house through the drizzling darkness, into the night.

Kelli changed into the dry clothes that she had packed to wear in the morning. She had lain back down on the bed, but her mind was too active to sleep. Again and again, she replayed the events of the night and all the emotions that she had experienced. The fact that Jace was worried about her, that he had run to her back door in total darkness, through a torrential storm—and even a possible tornado—to protect her, showed that he really cared for her.

Of course, she thought, he was simply being a good neighbor. Their roots went way back, and he was just being a Good Samaritan to his old friend since she didn't have television, radio, or internet service yet to warn her about an approaching tornado. Besides, he had checked on Mrs. Tanner, too, and mentioned that he always checked on her. He was just being neighborly, that was all.

However, there was the issue of his kiss. Its nature was not that of a friendly, neighborly kiss, but something more—much more. Kelli wondered if he'd felt the same tingling sensation course throughout his body that she had. She was probably just being silly. After all, they were practically raised together, and the bond of childhood friendship tends to remain with one for life. She tried to push all thoughts of Jace from her mind, and after much tossing and turning, she eventually fell asleep.

She awoke in the morning to sunshine streaming through the bare window of her bedroom. The storm was past, the sun was out, and she had spent her first night in her childhood home in a most memorable way. She planned to return to her apartment until her house was ready to move into. However, it had felt nice to stay here again.

She sat up in bed and rubbed her eyes as she looked around. It was then that she remembered the repetitive, ghostly girl sightings of her youth, and she was somewhat relieved to find that no repeat of that had taken place last night.

She decided that she had better get ready before Mr. Mills showed up for work, and she reached for her purse to retrieve her cell phone to check the time, but her phone was not in her purse. She didn't remember taking it out last night. She got up and looked around the house and found it lying on the kitchen counter. It had been such a wild, stormy night that she must have forgotten that she had taken the phone in there at some point.

She washed her face and brushed her hair before going outside to look around for any storm damage. Nothing appeared to be harmed, although numerous branches and limbs had fallen from trees which she dragged to the burn pile. She was so thankful that her house didn't suffer any structural damage from the high winds.

She checked Mrs. Tanner's house and yard, too, and knocked on her door, but she wasn't back from her daughter's house yet, Kelli decided after there was no answer. Her place looked fine with just some limbs being blown down, too, which Kelli hauled over to the burn pile in her own yard.

Mr. Mills was already at her house when Kelli dragged the last of the limbs from Mrs. Tanner's yard to her growing pile.

"Some storm last night, huh?" he asked. "I was afraid we were going to have us a twister, but the good Lord protected us."

Kelli agreed that the storm could have been so much worse than it was. It had been a close call, all right, but she was currently much more concerned about a different kind of storm. *The one that was beginning to brew in her heart.*

Chapter 8

The next few weeks were a blur as tile layers, roofers, floor refinishers and Mr. Mills worked magic on Kelli's house. Of course, she worked daily on all that she could do, as well. She painted all the walls, doors, cabinets, and moldings herself and felt such a sense of satisfaction from doing so. The kitchen looked better than Kelli could have ever imagined. It indeed looked very Old World, with the charming cabinet stain and paint, the wall wash that was ragged on with bits of gold and copper flecks, and the earthen tiles on the floor and countertops that had the look and feel of aged terra cotta. The finishing touch was the cabinet and drawer pulls which Kelli found at a local flea market and knew would be the accessory that pulled the room together. She planned to visit a nearby nursery and buy a large, potted palm to sit in the corner of the kitchen beside the table to complete the European feel.

Likewise, the bathroom was now functional with the floor and wall tile being finished, and the water turned back on. A new pedestal sink and matching toilet gave the former, tired bathroom a decidedly modern and upbeat feel. The walk-in shower was luxurious, compared to the previous chipped fiberglass tub, and the entire room looked nothing like the bathroom that had been here when she was a girl.

The home's original hardwood floors in the bedrooms, living room and hallway were stripped, buffed and polished back to their original luster. Kelli was thrilled with the gorgeous rich gleam of the wood, and it meant a lot to her to have it look like it must have when it was originally laid. She was thrilled with the way it all had turned out and had taken pictures with her phone and sent to her parents and brother. They could not believe how different it looked and congratulated her on all her hard work. That weekend the movers were going to load her furniture and belongings both at her apartment and the storage unit she had. They would work all day Saturday unloading, and she would enjoy taking her time to place everything just so. The upstairs loft still needed to be completed, as did the guest room and half bath, but Mr. Mills assured her that it would not be too messy for him to continue to work on these projects after she had moved in.

Since the night of the storm, she had not stayed overnight again at her house, but decided to wait until she actually moved in. She and Jace had gone to a movie once and grabbed a couple dinners at the diner after hectic days. They both had been so busy, and Jace had several emergency surgeries to contend with, in addition to his regular patients. He had never mentioned the kiss they had shared at her house on that stormy night, but rather, whenever they parted he would simply plant a chaste kiss on her cheek. Kelli reasoned that her heightened senses over the storm that night made her read more into the kiss than was actually there. She told herself to be glad that nothing more existed between them than friendship, because once that line was crossed, their strong bond of friendship that had been in existence since childhood could possibly be jeopardized.

And she didn't want that.

Jace knew that she had hired a moving crew for the upcoming weekend, and after that she would be living full-time at the house again.

Saturday morning dawned bright and clear, and it promised to be a gorgeous late spring day—a superb day for moving, Kelli happily noted. She had meticulously labeled the boxes according to what rooms they were to be placed in, so unloading was easy for the crew of three men. Kelli decided to tackle the kitchen first and was stacking stoneware dishes in the cupboards when Jace walked in behind her wearing jeans, a sweatshirt and sneakers. He was carrying an enormous picnic basket filled with chicken salad sandwiches, grapes, chips and drinks.

"Hi, Jace! What a nice surprise!" Kelli said, as she sat down the dishes and walked over to the basket he was holding. "And how sweet of you!" she added, as she opened the lid and peered inside.

"I figured you wouldn't stop for lunch," Jace said, opening her empty, new refrigerator and placing the sandwiches inside. "So now you have no excuse not to eat with me since everything is already prepared."

"As you can see, I don't have anything in there to fix yet, anyway," Kelli laughingly replied, nodding to the refrigerator. "I suppose that I'll make a run to the grocery store as soon as I'm unpacked."

"Not tonight, though," Jace said, closing the refrigerator door. "Mrs. Tanner has it all arranged for you and I to be her dinner guests tonight. She said it's her housewarming gift to you."

"You guys are so nice to me." Kelli looked as if she might cry. It was like returning home to family again after a twenty-year absence.

"There's no time for waterworks, now," Jace humorously retorted. "Let's get busy unpacking these boxes."

"You're staying to help?" she asked in amazement.

"Don't act so surprised. After all, what are friends for?"

Together they unpacked utensils, glasses, baking dishes, pots and pans and assorted other kitchen items all the while laughing and talking together. It made the job go so much faster and smoother having a friend to help pass the time with. Kelli was thankful for Jace and owed him a lot in return.

"When you get ready to move into your new house, it will be my chance to return the favor by helping you," she offered.

"Fair enough. Although after this week, the builders have to pull off my job to finish another one and don't plan on being back for weeks. The way they are working, it will be another ten years before I get to move in," Jace retorted.

"If it is as big as what I see beginning to be framed on that hill, it will take every bit that long," Kelli joked. "You're building a mansion!"

Jace seemed a little embarrassed as he looked away. "Just big enough for a family to run and play in someday without stepping on each other's toes."

"You must be planning on having a mighty large family. Just how many kids do you plan on having?" Kelli asked, enjoying teasing him.

"Probably at least a dozen," Jace answered, without missing a beat.

"Well, you'd better get busy and start finding a wife to help you meet that goal."

"I'm working on it, I'm working on it," replied Jace, glancing her way.

By early afternoon, the kitchen and bathroom boxes were unpacked, and Jace and Kelli decided to take a break and sat at the table to eat the lunch that Jace had packed for them. It was delicious, and Kelli didn't realize how hungry she was. The movers had very few questions for her during the day, other than the placement of the furniture, but the boxes were so clearly labeled that the job was a cinch for them. By the time Jace and Kelli were breaking for lunch the movers had the entire truck unloaded and were preparing to leave in the moving van. It was a very smooth process, and Kelli felt it was another good sign that she was doing the right thing by moving back here. Nothing had arrived broken—or worse, lost—and everything had a place in her sentimental home. It was the beginning of a new chapter in her life, a fresh page in an old book, full of exciting new potential.

After lunch Jace helped Kelli move a few large pieces of furniture that she had changed her mind about after the movers had unloaded them. He made sure that she could handle unpacking the smaller boxes alone, and then excused himself to make his rounds at the hospital before meeting her at Mrs. Tanner's house for dinner at seven o'clock that evening.

Kelli decided to hang the drapes in her bedroom first, since she would be sleeping there tonight, and tomorrow she would conquer the other rooms. She made her bed with fresh linens after that and then piddled around placing books and trinkets on her dresser and nightstand to create the perfect look in a room she loved so dearly. Late that afternoon she showered and dressed for dinner.

When Mrs. Tanner opened the door she was wearing an apron, and the most delicious aromas were coming from the kitchen. Jace arrived shortly after Kelli, and the three of them had a fantastic evening of visiting while enjoying the home-cooked country dinner Mrs. Tanner had prepared. They did more reminiscing, laughing and sharing stories of things that had occurred more than twenty years before. In a sense, they were family, and the three of them shared such a strong history and common bond. After dinner Mrs. Tanner remarked that she would love to see Kelli's house in its finished state.

"Why don't we walk over and let you see it now?" Kelli asked. "You'll have to step around a few boxes, but you can get an idea of the finished look."

Mrs. Tanner loved that idea. She had been over a few times while Kelli, Mr. Mills and others were working, bringing coffee or lemonade and cookies. The workers always looked forward to the freshly-baked goodies she would bring with her. She didn't want to get in their way and certainly not hamper their work, so she made a point of not going over as often as she would have liked, but still she definitely kept up-to-date with all the work that was taking place.

Jace led the way across Mrs. Tanner's backyard, holding back tree limbs for Kelli and Mrs. Tanner as he stepped into Kelli's back yard. Kelli opened the front door and stepped back to let Mrs. Tanner enter first. She heard her gasp and sigh as she said, "Oh honey, it is just beautiful."

Kelli gave them a tour of the house, leading them through each room and pointing out what had been done to them. She paused at the guest bedroom, explaining that more work was to be started in there and a half bath would be added. Mrs. Tanner praised Kelli's ability to see the end result in her mind from the hideous appearance of the rooms before.

"Would you care for coffee?" Kelli asked, after the tour. "I happen to have a coffeepot on the countertop, and I even know exactly where the cups are!"

"You young folks go ahead," Mrs. Tanner answered. "I'm afraid I've had enough excitement for one night." Then she wrapped her arms around both Kelli and Jace and gave them each a peck on the cheek. "Thank you so much for sharing dinner with me. I had a wonderful time with you and maybe we can make this a regular happening."

"Next time, dinner will be over here at my place," Kelli offered. "Just don't expect as delicious a meal as we had tonight. I could never cook as well as you do," she complimented Mrs. Tanner.

"Yes, you will, dear," Mrs. Tanner reassured. "It just takes lots of practice, and once you have a family, you will certainly get lots of that."

The three friends all shared a laugh, then Jace said, "If you don't mind, Kelli, I'd love to take you up on that offer of coffee. I'll walk Mrs. Tanner back to her house, first."

Mrs. Tanner tried to assure them that she could easily find her house safely in the dark, but Jace wouldn't hear of it and escorted her home. Within minutes he was back in Kelli's house, and they were sitting at the table waiting for the coffee to perk.

"So, now what do you plan on doing with all your extra time, since you've moved in?" Jace clasped his hands on the kitchen table in front of him.

Something between a sneer and a laugh escaped from Kelli. "As if there is nothing left to work on around here. Mr. Mills and I still have the guest room and half-bath to complete. And then there's the little loft up there," she nodded toward the small set of spiral stairs that led to the little open upstairs area. "I haven't decided what to do up there. Perhaps make it into a small library with a futon tucked into the corner for cozy reading. It's strange seeing stairs in this house since there were none when I lived here as a child. In fact, that small loft was actually a portion of the attic. "

Jace was studying the upper loft. "It does make a difference in the room. I actually like the change, and the little space has a window in it that overlooks your back yard."

"I know. I like it, too." She got up to pour the coffee and set the creamer and sugar on the table. "I also have another project in the works."

"What's that?"

Kelli poured the freshly-brewed coffee into each of their mugs. "My arabechia farm manager, Totseui, called me yesterday and was discussing some needed equipment for the future harvest. There are questions about storage capabilities and the need to rent additional space prior to the actual manufacturing process."

"Doesn't he, as your farm manager, handle all of this for you?" Jace asked.

"Ultimately, yes," Kelli answered. "But I make all of the decisions based upon both his recommendations and my own research of this herb. You must understand, Jace, that I bought this fledgling farm for a song and with no previous knowledge of the arabechia herb itself. It was a gamble but the price was right, and I learned that the herb's healing properties had caught the attention of some major pharmaceutical companies. For these reasons, I really felt that I couldn't go wrong. It has been my responsibility to learn all that I can about the medical benefits of arabechia, as well as its farming and harvesting methods, the manufacturing of it after harvesting, and then marketing it to the medical labs that are interested in it."

In the warm lighting from the glow of the kitchen lamp, Jace's eyes flickered with obvious admiration. "It sounds as if you've basically taught yourself everything about this subject, and that you continue to read and learn. That takes an extremely self-motivated, disciplined person, Kel, and I admire your determination in this business venture. I can't imagine how difficult it must be to oversee a farm from the other side of the world."

"That's another problem, Jace," said Kelli, as she leaned forward as if about to let him in on a dark secret. "I've never even been to this farm that I bought, never even set foot in Zambia, or anywhere else in Africa for that matter. I feel like I need to visit, and Totseui feels it would be a great help if we finally met and tackled some of these issues in person."

"So you're planning to fly to Zambia?" Jace asked incredulously. "When?"

"The sooner the better. I'm calling a travel agent in the morning to discuss the options." Kelli sipped her coffee and then sat the mug down, never taking her eyes from Jace's face. "Have you ever been to Zambia, Jace?"

"Of course, I travel there each summer," he jokingly retorted, as he stirred more cream into his steaming coffee. When he looked up, Kelli was staring intently at his face. Her eyes held his and they sat this way for a moment before Jace spoke. "So . . . what are you doing . . . inviting me to tag along?"

Kelli shook her head, as if trying to clear her thoughts. "No, I realize how silly that idea is. I'm sorry . . . I don't know what came over me. It's just that ever since I've moved back here again, it's like you are my family and I . . . just . . . well, I think of you as such."

A smile worked its way up to Jace's eyes. "I'm flattered, Kelli, really flattered. And I think visiting a strange, foreign land is just what I need right now. It sounds like a wonderful adventure."

72

Kelli's eyes lit up. "It does? Then you'll come along? Of course, we can schedule the trip to coincide with your vacation time—that is, if you even get a vacation." Her face suddenly looked worried as she contemplated how a busy cardiologist could ever possibly leave his patients and find time for pleasure.

"Yes, we get vacations, just like other people do. I'll just need to make sure that another doctor will be available to cover my patients during our time away." He smiled. "It will work with a little planning. Besides, I didn't have any vacation plans yet."

"Whoopee!" Kelli jumped up from her chair, danced over to Jace, and planted a kiss on his cheek. He sat there a for a second, then arose, grabbed her by the waist, pulled her close to his body, and kissed her firmly on the lips.

Chapter 9

Kelli slept soundly that night, her belly satiated by Mrs. Tanner's home-cooked meal and her heart happy at Jace's surprising willingness to travel across the globe with her. She dreamed about foreign lands, billowing fields of grain, and rain-kissed jungles, and when she awoke the sun was already streaming in her bedroom window. She yawned and stretched and once again proudly upheld her decision to move back to this state, this neighborhood, this house. It felt wonderful to wake up in one's childhood home again.

As she padded through the living room, she glumly saw that she had left the kitchen light on all night and silently chided herself to be less careless in the future. No longer receiving a salary, she had to learn to be more frugal and less wasteful, especially since she was trying to get a new business venture off the ground. This thought reminded her to later call the travel agent and discuss some travel arrangements.

By mid-morning, Kelli had begun pulling old wallpaper off the upstairs loft area. One of the owners that moved in after her family moved out had decided to add the loft and chose floral wallpaper for the area. After weeks of studying the area, Kelli decided that it would look better with a neutral coat of paint.

She took a break from ripping the paper to call the travel agent and learned that a flight could be booked in as early as two days. Luckily, she had obtained a passport when she bought her farm in Zambia, and Jace had obtained one several years earlier when he had traveled to Paris before he began medical school. Because of the extreme remoteness, it would take a couple days to reach the tiny town in Zambia using a combination of four different airplanes. The flight could be arranged at a much better price two weeks from now. Kelli thanked the travel agent and promised to call her back when she and Jace agreed upon a date. She then called

Jace's phone and left a brief message for him to call her after he came home from work regarding a departure date.

She was working up in the loft, pulling large pieces of the wallpaper off the wall, when she felt a small knob, similar to a cabinet pull, in the middle section of the back wall. Pulling the knob gently, a narrow door opened, and she found herself peering into darkness. She went downstairs to retrieve a flashlight and then went back up to the landing and again opened the small door, which completely blended into the wall since it was papered to match.

Beaming her flashlight through the opening, she waited for her eyes to adjust to the swath of light coming in from both an attic vent and an oval window which was almost completely encrusted with dust. She had to crouch down to walk through the doorway, but when she stood she found herself standing in the back portion of the attic of her old childhood home.

A wave of nostalgia washed over her as she recalled the last time she had set foot in this space. She was probably five or six years old and had followed her dad up here to carry down some Christmas decorations. Previous owners must have added this whimsical doorway when they opened up an extensive portion of the attic to make room for the loft area. About a fourth of the original attic was here, a considerable amount of useful storage space, Kelli delightfully discovered.

She spent the remainder of the day pulling and scraping all of the wallpaper completely off the upstairs area, while mentally planning what to store in the attic. Around six o'clock that evening there was a knock at her back door and Kelli peeked through the kitchen window to see Jace standing outside.

"Hi," Kelli said, opening the door to let him in. "I was expecting you to call tonight. You didn't need to make a special trip over here," she added, tucking a stray strand of blonde hair behind her ear.

"Don't be silly, all I had to do was walk across the road," grinned Jace, as he leaned down to plant a friendly kiss on her cheek. "So, your message said you spoke with a travel agent this morning. What's the plan?"

Kelli led him in to the kitchen. "Flight arrangements can be scheduled for as early as two weeks from now. I need to know what would be a good time for you to go."

Jace thought for a moment. "Two weeks is an acceptable amount of time for me to make arrangements to be gone. This afternoon I talked with Dr. Nehrow, the other cardiologist, and he is willing to cover for me. How long do you think we'll be gone?" Jace asked, as he pulled out a kitchen chair and sat down at the table.

Kelli poured two glasses of ice tea and joined Jace at the table. "According to the travel agent, it will take a couple of days to get there and a couple more to come home. I'd like ample time in Zambia to visit the farm, work with Totseui on some manufacturing and harvesting ideas, and discuss the needed equipment."

Kelli flashed a timid smile toward Jace. "Of course, I think it would be silly to travel that far and not do a little sightseeing while we're there. We should look at being gone around ten days. Is that too long for you?"

"That's fine with me," said Jace. "After all, if it takes that long to get there, we'd better do everything we need and want to do while we are there."

Kelli agreed and they decided upon two weeks from the coming weekend to depart. Kelli promised to call the travel agent in the morning and book their flights. Then they chatted about each other's day, and Kelli told him about finding the surprise doorway to the attic. Jace wanted to see it, so they walked up to the landing, and Kelli pointed out the small attic doorway which was much more visible now, having been stripped of its wallpaper.

Jace liked the space and smiled at her. "You work all the time. A trip to Zambia, even if it is under the auspices of work, is just what you need." He started down the stairs to the back door and then stopped.

"How about going out to dinner with me tomorrow evening?" he asked.

"How about eating a pot of spaghetti over here?" countered Kelli. "I can simmer the sauce on the stove while I paint up here. Besides, I'll probably have paint all over me and you would undoubtedly be embarrassed to be seen with me."

"I would never be embarrassed to be seen with you, regardless of how much paint you're wearing." Kelli felt his eyes sweeping over her. "But, if you're sure it's not too much trouble, spaghetti would be delicious."

"Great. Maybe, I'll have the trip information all ready, too."

Jace stopped at the door and wrapped his arms around Kelli's waist. "I respect you, Kel and want to be clear about the fact that separate rooms on the trip are fine with me."

Kelli's eyes twinkled. "I've already planned for that, of course," she said. "But, thank you for being a gentleman. And a terrific friend," she added.

Jace leaned down and kissed her sweetly, softly on the lips. Then he murmured in her ear, "However, I've heard that Zambia is an extremely romantic place, what with all the lions and giraffes and jungles and . . . ."

He was shushed by Kelli wrapping her arms around his neck and kissing him back. She wondered what she was getting herself into.

* * * * * * * *

77

The next day began with a call to the travel agent where round trip flights for Jace and herself were booked. They would depart from Fayetteville, change planes in Atlanta, fly to New York for a short layover, and then stop in Rome to refuel, before arriving in Lusaka, Zambia. From there Totseui would pick them up at the airport and shuttle them to the small, farming community of Mambashaiu, about three hours away via a jeep. They would be staying at a guest lodge nearby.

Totseui was thrilled that Kelli was finally coming to Zambia to see her farm in person. He had many issues and ideas to discuss with her, and obviously decisions were better made when the owner was present on site.

After the planning was finalized, Kelli set about painting the walls of the loft and landing area. After priming the area, she was able to apply one coat of paint. While it was drying, Kelli prepared the spaghetti sauce, leaving it to gently simmer. She barely had time to shower, doing her best to scrub off the paint from her skin, and dress in khaki pants and a tangerine pheasant blouse before Jace arrived carrying a bouquet of pink tulips.

"They're beautiful," Kelli gushed, wrapping her arms around Jace's neck. "Come in and I'll get a vase for these. How was your day?"

Jace followed her into the kitchen. "Hectic. I was awakened at 3:30 this morning with a call from the hospital and had to perform an emergency triple bypass on a 64-year old man." He paused, sniffing the delicious aroma wafting from the stove. "Mmmmm, I could get used to coming home to this. Usually, I curl up with a bowl of cold cereal and then fall asleep on the couch still clutching my bowl."

"You poor thing," crooned Kelli, in her best sarcastic tone as she stirred the simmering pot. "A handsome, young doctor like you should be entitled to an active social life in the evenings." Then growing serious she asked, "Are you sure you can get away for ten whole days, Jace? You have such a busy schedule, and so many people depend on you."

Jace hugged her gently. "Now don't start worrying about me. As I've said, Dr. Nehow has agreed to cover for me. Doctors need time to recharge their batteries, and I've not taken time off since I came here. I'm really looking forward to this trip." He took a spoon from a drawer and dipped it into the spaghetti sauce, holding it in front of him to cool. "Speaking of, did you get our flights booked?"

"I certainly did," Kelli answered and shared all the flight information with him. "Our tickets should arrive in the mail in the next day or two."

Jace nodded, licking his lips from tasting the sauce. "This is so good, Kel." He put the spoon in the sink and leaned against the counter. "You know, you should be as exhausted as I am since it looked like you were working all night yourself. I saw the light on in the attic when I was leaving for the hospital this morning."

"What are you talking about? I slept like a baby all night." Kelli paused, trying to grasp what Jace had just said. "Besides, there is no light in the attic."

"That little oval window was all aglow and . . ." he stopped talking and studied her eyes. "Come to think of it, I've never seen a light on in that window before. Are you sure there is no light up there?"

"I couldn't find a switch. I've had to use a flashlight whenever I go up there." Kelli's eyes darted around nervously. "Are you sure you saw a light? Maybe it was the reflection from the moon or a streetlight or something."

Jace was shaking his head. "No, it was definitely a light." He started for the stairs. "Let's go take a look," he said, leading the way. Kelli grabbed a flashlight and followed him.

The small door in the loft area was shut tight. "Be careful, the paint may not be totally dry," warned Kelli.

Jace carefully pulled the door open and slipped inside, reaching behind him for Kelli's hand. Kelli grabbed hold of his strong hand while simultaneously turning on the flashlight and beaming it all around.

"Let's start on this wall inside the door," directed Jace. "Let me see the light a moment."

Kelli handed him the flashlight, and he slowly beamed it up and down the attic wall beside the door, continuing to do so in a sweeping manner until they had searched all of the walls of the attic.

"See, there's not a switch up here," said Kelli, still holding Jace's hand.

Jace shone the flashlight thoroughly around the unfinished attic roof. "There's not even a light fixture up here. And judging from the lack of wiring to the attic's ceiling, there never has been."

He led Kelli back to the small door, stepped aside, and let her emerge into the loft area first, before stepping out and closing the door behind him. They descended the stairs quietly into the living room, and Kelli motioned for him to have a seat on the couch.

"What are we to make of this?" Kelli wondered aloud, as she sat down next to Jace.

Jace turned to look at her. "Have you had any reason to believe that your little friend knows you are back?"

Chapter 10

Kelli was too stunned to think for a moment when she realized that Jace was referring to the apparition of the little girl she used to see as a child in this house. She shook her head. "Don't tell me you think a ghost is responsible for a light being on in the attic last night?" she finally managed to utter.

"It's not that absurd of a thought, Kel. After all, this house has a history of being haunted. Have there been any other unexplained incidents since you've come back?"

Kelli continued shaking her head no.

Jace kept speaking his thoughts aloud. "Any sort of what would be classified as paranormal activity, you know, hearing footsteps, noises, voices, objects being moved, lights turned on or off . . . ."

"Wait!" Kelli interrupted. "There have been a couple of instances like that. Once, I went to retrieve my cell phone from my purse and couldn't find it. Later I discovered it on the kitchen counter. I didn't remember using it in there."

Kelli tried to think clearly, rubbing her temples in concentration. "Another time I woke up and discovered that I'd left a light on all night. Deep down, I knew that I hadn't left any lights on, as I always double-check before going to bed, and anyway, I scolded myself for being careless. But I didn't attribute either of these incidents to the ghost. Why would she play tricks on me and not just make herself visible to me like she always did in the past?"

Jace shook his head and shrugged. "You said that you always saw the apparition coming out of the kitchen. How many times have you arisen during the night and walked through that area since you've been back?"

"That's a very good point, Jace," Kelli mused, deep in thought. "None that I can recall."

"Maybe you should set your alarm for a specific hour during the night, and go get yourself a glass of water in the kitchen—in the dark, of course—and see if she appears to you again."

"I suppose," sighed Kelli.

Jace scooted over on the couch and wrapped his arms around her. "Are you okay with possibly sharing this house with your ghost for the second time in your life?"

"I don't know if it will be the same this time. I mean, I'm a grown woman, no longer a child, and her spirit is probably still that of a young girl. Will she want anything to do with a grown woman?" She looked into Jace's concerned eyes. "And if she still resides here, will she even recognize me as the same young girl who once lived here many years ago?"

Jace gave her shoulder a firm squeeze. "I'm no authority on the paranormal, and I don't have answers to any of those questions. I suppose only time will reveal the answers. In the meantime," he said, gently touching the tip of her nose with his fingertip, "I think we should pay close attention to any event that seems unusual or abnormal."

"So, now we can add sleuthing to the added list of projects that you have become involved with since I moved back. You're going to be sorry you ever saw me again," laughed Kelli, rising from the couch. "You can forget about having an interesting and active social life. All your free time is going to be spent searching for ghosts and accompanying me on impromptu flights to Africa."

Jace stood up, too, and faced Kelli, then took her hands in his own. "Believe me when I say that there is nothing in this world that I would rather be doing."

He leaned down and brushed his lips against her cheek, her chin, before landing on her mouth. The kiss began as one of affection but grew much bolder, igniting sparks of passion between them.

Kelli reached up and wrapped her arms around his neck and responded with such willingness that she stunned herself. She was the one to pull back abruptly. She licked her lips and smoothed down her hair, but not before he noticed the desire in her eyes that matched his own.

"Let's go eat that spaghetti dinner," she suggested, her voice husky, as she led him to the kitchen on unsteady legs.

Dinner was an extremely pleasant time of talking, sharing and laughing as they discussed plans for their upcoming trip to Zambia. Kelli was happy for the opportunity to mix business with pleasure, and she owed a great deal of gratitude to Jace for agreeing to accompany her on the trip. They talked about what they hoped to see and experience while they were there, and Kelli remarked that she was compiling a list of ideas that she wanted to share with Totseui. She was eagerly anticipating meeting him in person, and at last seeing the farm that she had purchased. The thought of her being the owner of an African farm still seemed a bit absurd and made her hope that she hadn't lost complete control of her sanity when she had made the purchase.

Jace left around nine that evening saying he had early rounds to make the next morning. He gave her a hug before he left, but he didn't kiss her again. Kelli found herself surprised that she was disappointed by this. She was the one who was holding back, confused by her feelings for him, not wanting to risk disturbing the strong bond they'd shared their entire life. She knew that if they ever crossed over the line of friendship to romance, there would be no turning back. And if things didn't work out romantically between them, their friendship would be forever altered, possibly even ruined. She valued their strong bond of friendship too much to ever sacrifice the possibility that it could be weakened or destroyed by going beyond being platonic friends with him.

After changing into her gown, Kelli made sure that all the doors were locked, and all the lights were off except for her bedside lamp, and then she reached over and set her alarm for 12:30 a.m. She planned to do what Jace had suggested and walk into the hallway off the kitchen in an attempt to see her ghost girl. It seemed as if the moment her head hit the pillow, she was deep asleep.

Meanwhile, across the road, Jace was tossing and turning in his bed, despite being exhausted. His day had begun so early with performing an arduous surgery, but it had ended on a perfect note by having a quiet dinner with Kelli. He enjoyed each moment spent with her, and he found that being alone with her relaxed him more than anything else he could do. He knew there was a powerful, shared chemistry between them because each time he meant to give her a friendly peck it would grow into something much more. He could usually feel a slight hesitancy and restraint on Kelli's part, but not tonight. Tonight her urgency had matched his.

But then she had flippantly suggested they eat dinner, as if they had not just shared a passionate kiss, as if nothing had happened at all. Maybe she didn't have any romantic feelings for him, Jace considered. Maybe she couldn't get past the image of him as a kid. But as his mind replayed tonight's kiss, he had no doubt that she had seen him as desirable, as well.

The high-pitched, staccato beeps of the alarm clock on her nightstand woke Kelli with a start. It took a split-second for her to groggily remember why an alarm was sounding in the middle of the night. She got out of bed, grabbed her robe, and walked out of the bedroom toward the small hallway off of the kitchen.

Her heart was beating wildly as if in anticipation of seeing *her* again. She gradually quieted her footsteps and then, in the pitch black of the night, turned her head slowly to the left, half afraid of what she might see. She stopped outside the kitchen doorway, waiting and watching, while her eyes adjusted to the darkness.

But there was nothing. No sighting of the little girl.

Kelli felt a little deflated, yet at the same time more than a tad relieved. She found herself dreading the impending encounter, instead of just accepting it as she had done as a child. She decided to go ahead and get a drink of water while she was up, before returning to bed.

A beautiful spring morning greeted Kelli when she woke up. Birds were chirping in the trees outside her bedroom, and the sun was just spreading her golden fingers across the eastern horizon. Mr. Mills was coming again today, and Kelli was making a mental list of all that needed to be accomplished.

Deciding that a cup of fresh, hot coffee would help jolt her senses, she made her way to the kitchen and discovered that the lamp on the counter was on, casting a soft glow across the still-dim room. Kelli stopped suddenly, her hand covering her mouth in an attempt to quiet the small shriek she let out. There was no light on when she went to bed, she'd make sure of it, and there was certainly no lamp on in the kitchen when she'd gone in there during the night.

With trembling legs she walked over and turned off the lamp. She wished Jace were here to provide a plausible explanation. There *had* to be one, she was sure. Maybe he had stopped by this morning on his way to the hospital and didn't want to wake her. Of course, there was the possibility that she had sleep-walked. She made coffee and then went outside to sit on the patio and clear her head.

Mr. Mills arrived promptly at nine, the back of his ancient Toyota pickup filled with saws, toolboxes, and lumber. "Mornin'," he nodded, tipping the bill of his weathered ball cap. "Sure is a lovely day to be outside. Hard to believe in a couple of months it'll be hotter than blazes around here."

"I never remembered horribly hot summer days as a child in Arkansas," Kelli recalled. "Now, however, people have cautioned me about the summer's dreadful humidity and heat."

"When you walk outside in August, it'll be like walking into an oven," he warned. "The humidity will take your breath away." He fastened his tool belt around his waist. "When you were a young 'un, you probably kept cool with popsicles and swimming, huh?"

"You got that right. All of us kids in the neighborhood did just that," nodded Kelli. She smiled to herself remembering the fun times spent here with friends.

"Well, it's actually hotter now than it used to be, in my opinion," offered Mr. Mills, swinging the toolbox under his arm as he followed Kelli inside.

Kelli didn't know exactly how to ask the question that weighed heavily on her mind, so she just swallowed hard and let it out. "Mr. Mills, is it possible that the wiring in the house could have gotten sort of, I don't know, mixed up around here during the remodeling process?"

Mr. Mills sat down his toolbox and looked at her. "What do ya mean, mixed up?"

"Well, just that . . . possibly . . . lights could go on or off without anybody being in the room to turn them on or off?" She looked sheepishly at the floor, realizing how incredibly dumb that question sounded.

Mr. Mills just laughed and shook his head as he headed back out the door to retrieve more supplies. "No, that there is not a wiring problem." As the door closed behind him, Kelli heard him chortling and mumbling something under his breath about it sounding more like a ghost problem.

She decided to drop the subject and not even mention to Jace about awaking to find the lamp turned on in the kitchen. If he specifically asked her, then she would tell him, but she made up her mind to keep quiet about the matter from now on. The ghost from her past was something that had always intrigued her, and if the past was meant to repeat itself in the future, so be it. She'd find an answer somehow, someway, but she was not going to worry about it.

The week passed quickly. Mr. Mills worked every day, and Kelli kept busy running errands for him at the hardware store or lumber yard. Whenever he finished a particular area, she was right behind him painting it. He was very precise in his measurements and extremely picky in his work, which provided fabulous results, despite his occasional moodiness which often accompanies such a trait.

Jace had called her a few times during the week, and they had gone to a restaurant for dinner over the weekend. They would depart on their trip the next Saturday morning, and they both were looking forward to it. They had discussed what to pack and since it would be in the 80's during the day, they decided shorts and t-shirts would be practical, with jeans and a light jacket for the evenings when the temperature would drop into the 50's.

During one of their phone calls, Jace suddenly remembered something. "Did you try that nighttime experiment," he asked, "where you were going to set your alarm for the middle of the night, and go into the kitchen?" They had both been so busy lately that he had not even remembered to ask her.

"I did," Kelli answered. "And I saw nothing." She hesitated before going further, as if she couldn't decide if she should divulge anything else.

Jace could hear the reluctance in her voice and sensed that she was withholding something. "But . . .?" he pressed.

"But what?" Kelli asked innocently.

"Is there something else?"

"Well, it was probably nothing, but the next morning when I walked into the kitchen, the lamp on the counter was turned on. And I am 100 percent positive that there was no light on when I returned to bed that night."

Jace let out a low whistle. "That answers our question, Kelli. She's still there."

Chapter 11

It was still dark outside early Saturday morning when Jace pulled his car into Kelli's driveway. As he opened the car door, he looked up at the sky and took a moment to admire the millions of stars glittering above him. It promised to be a nice day with clear skies which meant excellent flying weather, for the first leg of their journey, anyway. He had never traveled so far away before, and the anticipation of this trip fluttered in his stomach like butterflies. He knocked softly on the back door, but didn't need to, because Kelli was watching for him, and her hand was already turning the doorknob before he finished knocking. She was wearing a buttery yellow cotton dress with a cream-colored sweater tied loosely around her neck. Her blonde hair lay in waves around her shoulders.

"I've got all my luggage right here," she said, nodding toward the one large and two small suitcases sitting beside the door.

"You're kidding, right?" joked Jace. "You mean you can pack for ten days with as little luggage as this? Most women would need this many bags just for their shoes."

"I don't see us attending many social events in Zambia, Jace. Hiking boots and sandals should pretty much fit the bill."

He stepped closer and put his arms around her waist. "I'm so looking forward to this, Kelli. Thanks for inviting me along." He leaned down and kissed her gently on the mouth. She kissed him back which promptly caused her heart to beat erratically.

She walked through her house a final time to double-check everything. She had lent a spare key to Mrs. Tanner who had promised to keep an eye on her place. She had her phone number if any concerns should arise, though Kelli warned her that many places she would be would probably not have cell service. The guest lodge where they planned to stay would be able to take messages though, so she had given her that number as well. Of course, her parents had the numbers also, and though they worried about her traveling so far, they were relieved to learn that Jace would be with her. He was like a part of their family, and they felt much safer knowing that Kelli had him as a neighbor again, too. Although in their mind's eye, he was still thought of as a young boy riding a bike with their son and daughter. They had not yet seen him as a grown adult.

Passengers were beginning to fill the airport when Jace and Kelli arrived. They checked their luggage and, after locating their gate number, visited a gift shop where Jace bought a daily paper and some coffee. Kelli also purchased a couple paperback novels to read both on the plane and while in Zambia, though she doubted she would have much time to read after they arrived.

Their flight was on time, and before they knew it, they had landed in Atlanta, changed planes after a brief layover and were headed for New York. The layover there would be for a few hours and would give them ample time to stretch their legs and walk around the airport for a while. Kelli and Jace sat together on each flight. They chatted, watched a movie, and read. Jace napped during some of the flight. They flew much of the night over the Atlantic and landed in Rome to refuel, but here passengers did not have to change planes. Still, most people welcomed the opportunity to stretch and use the restroom. A couple toddlers who had boarded the plane in New York awoke and were playfully running up and down the aisles of the plane while their weary mother smiled at the other passengers with apologetic eyes.

The final leg of their journey took them south from Rome to Africa. From the window of the plane, they could see a vast expanse of woodlands, and about that time the pilot came over the intercom announcing that they were flying over teak forests. Rich, fertile farmlands were scattered throughout the Congo River basin. Golden patches seen from the air were actually fields of maize, an export crop of Zambia. Soon, the plane began its slow descent toward the Lusaka International Airport.

"I can't wait to meet Totseui and finally see my farm," squealed Kelli, as she looked out the windows at the foreign country around her. They were landing in Lusaka, a highly populated city, and it did not resemble the secluded African villages in Kelli's mind. Totseui had told her that he would meet them at the airport and then drive them to the remote village where the farm was located, a few hours away.

After the plane landed, Jace and Kelli grabbed their carry-on bags from the overhead bin and made their way into the airport. It felt wonderful to finally stretch and walk for more than several feet at a time. There were people of all nationalities milling around. Some people were embracing loved ones who were either coming or going, while others were searching for friends. It was a common sight shared in thousands of airports around the world.

"Totseui said he would be holding a sign for us," Kelli said, as she scanned the area. There were many people, and so they kept walking among the crowd, all the while searching for a man holding a sign. Finally, they saw a slim, dark-skinned man wearing a straw hat standing to their right, with a large poster board sign bearing the crudely-written words, "Welcome Kelli and Jace." He was looking intently at each couple who walked by in an attempt to recognize his arriving visitors. It was difficult for both parties, since neither had any idea of what the other looked like. Kelli made a mental note that it would have been more helpful had they provided a photo or at least some type of physical description to one another prior to their arrival.

"There he is!" Kelli excitedly called, pointing to Totseui and turning in his direction. Jace followed, carrying their bags while dodging throngs of people.

Kelli stopped in front of the man of medium height, pointed to the sign and smiled. "Totseui?" she asked.

He had already begun nodding his head vigorously, while smiling broadly and shaking Kelli's hand. "Yes, yes," he said in English. "You Kelli?"

She nodded yes, and he hugged her, a huge smile still etched on his weathered face. "This is Jace," Kelli said, introducing her friend after Totseui's welcoming embrace.

"So nice meet you," Totseui said, shaking Jace's hand. "Come, let us get luggage."

They followed Totseui through the crowded lobby to the baggage claim area and retrieved their luggage after a short wait. Totseui then showed them where to do all the necessary paperwork, including visiting the bank with bureau de change located right in the airport. They exchanged some money for Zambian kwacha, the unit of money in Zambia. They had no trouble communicating with the workers, since most of them spoke English. Kelli recognized many languages being spoken around her, including German, French, Russian and English. She quickly learned that a language she was predominately hearing was Bemba and Tonga, which are two popular languages in Zambia. After everything was finished, Totseui looked at them and smiled again. His face had had a continual smile plastered on it since they arrived. "All ready?"

"I believe we are, Totseui. Let's go." They followed him out of the airport and into the warm air. It had a tropical feel to it, and they noticed an entirely different smell to the region. He led them through the parking lot to a muddy, white ancient jeep that was parked on the far side.

"Here we are," Totseui announced, placing their luggage in the back. Jace helped Kelli step up into the passenger side and then climbed into the back among the luggage.

Totseui, still smiling, reached up to the visor, pulled out a pair of sunglasses and put them on. "Get ready, it take a few hour to get there."

They pulled out of the parking lot onto East Great Road, the main route to and from the airport. "You have good trip?" Totseui asked them and they both shared information about the plane layovers, changes, movies, books and food. They amused him with tales of fellow passengers, and all in all, how it had been a very pleasant—albeit long—trip.

Totseui gave them a brief history of Zambia, explaining that Lusaka is both the capital and the largest city of that country. Most of the population is concentrated around Lusaka. "We be leaving the crowds," he explained. "You not see this many people where we go."

He turned off the main highway and began traveling southwest, toward the small village where Kelli's farm was located. After leaving the paved roads around the airport, they had soon turned onto gravel roads, rough but wide enough for two cars to pass. A bit later, the roads became smaller, tighter, and bumpier with massive potholes dotting the way. The jeep splashed through mud and angrily bumped over the numerous rocks scattered amid the road. Kelli clung to the dashboard for dear life and turned toward Totseui. "I see why you drive a jeep," she said. "A car would never make it on this road."

"No, car would not work." Totseui agreed. "You need four wheels."

Kelli nodded, understanding that he meant four-wheel drive. She turned around to check on Jace and found him smiling at her, while grabbing at the luggage that surrounded him in an attempt to keep them from falling out. He gave her a sexy wink, and Kelli returned his smile, thinking what a lucky woman she was.

It was nearing dusk when the jeep turned onto another rutted, dirt road, and Totseui explained that this road led to Mambashai, the tiny settlement that was their destination. Small huts made from baked mud and with thatched roofs sat in clusters along the sides of the road, while young children, dressed in mismatched Western attire watched wide-eyed as they approached. They recognized Totseui's jeep, for they began

93

running toward it. Waving to them, Totseui reached over to the glove box and brought out a handful of candy which he then tossed out the window as they drove by. Kelli looked back and watched the delighted children running over and picking up the candy, as if it had been tossed out along a parade route. She looked over at Totseui who once again had both hands on the steering wheel.

"My little friends," he explained with a shy grin.

They passed women, dressed in brightly-colored sarongs, chatting with one another in cluttered yards, their babies comfortably slung, papoose-style, around their backs. Another woman was walking along the side of the road carrying a vessel of river water on her head. In a yard to their right sat an elderly woman pounding grain with a mortar and pestle. Elephant grass and eucalyptus trees dotted the landscape, which was surprisingly green and tropical. The area certainly was not anything similar to the hot, dry African landscape images that Kelli had conjured up in her mind. Many such areas existed throughout Africa, but here in the basin of the Zambezi River, the land was rich and fertile, the landscape green and lush.

"It appears to be a very poor village," Kelli observed aloud. Most of the houses they were passing would be classified as little more than shacks in the United States.

"In the 1970's Zambia slid into poverty when their principal export, copper, declined around the world. Many men are employed in the mines. Here, we have cobalt, lead and zinc mines, besides copper." Totseui shifted gears, slowing the Jeep down, as a goat ambled onto the road, causing Jace to chuckle in the backseat. "Most peoples who live in this region are subsistence farmers. Under last owner, your farm gave jobs to about nine local men. But with your plans, it will give work to many more."

Kelli liked the thought of helping the locals here. Perhaps with her proposed expansion and manufacturing plans, her farm could provide more families with money to live, maybe even have a better lifestyle.

Ever the doctor, Jace questioned Totseui about the availability of medical assistance for the local villagers.

"No hospital for long way," he answered. "But the village has two doctors with Peace Corps." He paused a moment and then remembered a precaution. "Cholera and dysentery are common to Zambia, especially during the rainy season from November to April. Drink or use only water which come in bottle or boil it," he cautioned.

Jace and Kelli thanked him and assured him that they would do so, although both had come prepared with the knowledge to do so already.

The jeep bounced along before it slowed and turned right onto a gravel driveway that led to the lodge. Actually, the driveway appeared to be no more than a mere band of dirt in the middle of an expansive field of green. Far ahead, situated in a lush meadow, glowed lantern lights hung on the exterior of the lodge. As they drove closer, they saw that the lodge consisted of one small office building constructed of timbers and was surrounded by several cabins that looked like tree houses built on stilts. Each cabin's exterior consisted of rough-hewn local wood and sat atop thick, sturdy logs which rose from the ground. Thatched roofs topped each hut, and Kelli remarked that she felt as if she had stepped onto the set of *Swiss Family Robinson*.

Totseui parked in front of the office, and he, Kelli, and Jace climbed out, stretching their legs after the long, jarring ride from the airport. The evening air was warm, and a small breeze ruffled their hair. Everything felt different to Kelli and Jace. The air had a different smell, a different feel, and the night noises were new to their ears.

They followed Totseui inside and waited beside him as he spoke in Bemba to the young man behind the desk, who then came around the counter and bowed slightly before them, his broad smile revealing a missing front tooth. Totseui introduced the man as Answai. They returned the smile, and then relied on Totseui to interpret for them.

Before long the paperwork was signed and finished, and the young man led them outside and stopped in front of the third cabin from the office. He climbed the dozen or so log steps that led to the front door, unlocked it, then swung it open for his guests. All three followed him up, and then Totseui explained that either Jace or Kelli would be staying in this cabin, and the other would be staying in cabin four, which was located next door.

The walls were comprised of wood, as were the floor and ceiling. A large, carved log headboard adorned the front of the bed which bore a bright, floral-patterned cotton bedspread, and a nightstand that matched the headboard sat next to it. On the opposite wall sat a large dresser, and it was also carved from the same wood as the headboard and nightstand. The window, which had no pane of glass, was wide open, and some blinds made from what appeared to be grass cloth hung over it and could be raised or lowered for privacy. In case of rainy or cooler weather, a wooden panel could swing over the window, but it was currently hooked outside on the cabin itself. The rainy season was over and it never got cold, so there was no need for it now. There was a small bathroom, and the fact that indoor plumbing was even available relieved Kelli. A small toilet, sink, and shower stall were tightly squeezed into the tiny room. And the cabins all had electricity, too.

Sitting on top of the dresser was a wicker basket containing fresh papaya, kumquats and plantains. A dozen bottles of water sat next to it. Kelli was sure that this act of hospitality was arranged for by Totseui, and she shot him a grateful look.

Jace sat down two of Kelli's suitcases. "If this suite meets your approval, then please have the honors," he clowned. "I'll take the next one."

96

"This is nice, very nice," Kelli answered, looking around at the somewhat crude surroundings, but absolutely loving the ethnic feel of it. She looked over at Jace and couldn't resist teasing him a bit. "However, I'm going over to the next cabin to make sure you are not receiving any kind of special treatment." She bounced past him, following Totseui and Answai out the door, as Jace playfully swatted her backside.

Jace's cabin was identical to hers except the bedspread had a bold, paisley print on it. Answai told them to let him know if they needed anything, and that he would be in the office. Kelli wondered how they would communicate with him since Totseui had interpreted all of this information to them. He then smiled, bowed again, and left to return to the office.

Jace sat his luggage down beside the dresser and motioned to the bed for the others to have a seat. "Let's try some of this fruit," he suggested, picking up the basket and examining the contents.

Totseui remained standing, shaking his head. "No, no, this food for you hungry travelers. I know you are tired and need to rest, so I am going home." As farm manager, he lived in a small house on Kelli's farm. "What time do I pick you up in the morning?" he asked her.

"How about 8:00?" Kelli said. "However, I'm so excited to finally get to see my farm that I don't know if I'll be able to sleep tonight."

Totseui understood what she meant. "It only about 15 minutes away. I take you there tonight, but it will be too dark to see," he shrugged his shoulders ruefully.

"That's all right, Totseui," Kelli answered gratefully, walking over to stand beside him. "I've waited this long, what's one more night? Thank you for picking us up at the airport and bringing us here to this lovely lodge."

He had given up an entire day to meet them and shuttle them around. Although today was the first time that Kelli actually had met him in person, they had spoken many, many times over the phone, so she felt as if she had known him for a long time. He bid them good night and then left them alone in Jace's cabin.

Kelli sat down on the bed, and Jace joined her, bringing over the fruit basket and a bottle of water. She was extremely thirsty, she realized, remembering that they had not had a drink since the plane ride. She took a long sip of water, looking at him over the bottle. "So, what do you think of Zambia, so far?"

"Well, other than the bumpy jeep ride, we really haven't had a chance to form any opinions. But, once we got away from the airport and the big city of Lusaka, the landscape was really beautiful. I'm looking forward to our exploring the region together."

"So am I," agreed Kelli. "And I can't wait to finally visit my farm in the morning."

"I know you can't," said Jace, peeling a papaya and handing her a piece. "Do you even know what an arabechia plant looks like?" he asked with mischievous eyes.

"I've just seen pictures. But I'll be an expert by the time we leave this place." Kelli swallowed the papaya. "These are delicious."

"Yes, they are. However, I'm sure their flavor is boosted by the fact that we are two hungry and exhausted travelers in a strange village."

Kelli giggled, looking around the cabin. "These cabins actually look like little huts. When Totseui said he'd made arrangements for us at a local lodge, I envisioned a lavish log cabin with comfortable, overstuffed chairs that encircled a huge stone fireplace. And it would have been nice to have had a hot tub on the deck."

Jace laughed at her luxurious description. "These little cabins will give us more of a feel for the area." He scooted closer and wrapped his arms around Kelli. "I'm finally halfway around the world with you, all alone in an African hut, and there's not even a television on the premises. Whatever are we going to do to entertain ourselves?"

Kelli playfully poked him in the ribs and then leaned in for a kiss. Jace simply groaned and pulled her closer.

Chapter 12

Kelli awakened to the steady ringing of the wind-up alarm clock she had brought with her. She didn't know where she was for a moment, and it took a while for her senses and her mind to adjust to the surroundings. She didn't dare trust herself to wake up on her own and miss her appointment with Totseui. Her sense of time was all out of sorts, and jet lag would surely catch up with her and Jace today.

Jace. As she said his name she recalled the events of the previous night. She had quickly left his cabin after spending half an hour kissing him and lying in his arms. She left while she still was in her right mind. She hadn't dared to stay for fear that they would cross the line and do something that they both would regret this morning. He was her childhood friend, they'd been best buddies for heaven's sake, and she didn't ever want to lose that tight bond. One flippant night in an exotic African hut might cause her to take leave of her senses and change all that. Forever. She was much too prudent for that, too sensible. However, Jace was almost irresistible last night. And being the practical, reasonable woman that she was, Kelli was certain that the remote hideaway they were at only helped to romanticize the situation further.

Once she was back in her own cabin last night, she had trouble unwinding from the long trip and falling asleep, even though she was exhausted. Not only was she feeling edgy from Jace, but all the strange, new noises of the Zambian night captivated her attention and kept sleep at bay. She heard the chirps of peculiar insects and the calls of wild animals in the nearby jungle. She didn't know if they were monkeys, leopards, hyenas or what, but she had found herself lying very still and listening, remembering that there was nothing between her bed and the ground outside, other than the thin flap of grass cloth over the window. She tried not to think about exotic snakes, lizards or other reptiles climbing in through the open window during the night, but nonetheless found herself looking under her bed and around the floor before putting her feet down this morning as a precaution.

Squeezing into the small cubicle of a shower, she managed to bump her funny bone twice and hit her knee once. Although it was space-challenged, the shower felt wonderful and the water was actually almost hot. She dried her hair, gathering it into a loose knot at the back of her head, leaving small, curly, blonde tendrils hanging down. What was the use of fixing her hair, anyway, she thought. They would be riding in an open jeep again today and touring the farm outdoors. She dressed in comfortable blue jeans and a yellow cotton t-shirt and then decided she'd better go see if Jace was up and ready for Totseui to arrive. Perhaps they would have time for breakfast first, she thought as her stomach growled. They had not checked to see if the lodge served breakfast, and she was seriously hoping that it did.

She saw no indication that Jace was up yet, as she walked down the outside stairs of her hut and looked over toward his hut. She climbed his stairs and knocked loudly on his teakwood door. In a few seconds the door swung open widely, revealing Jace standing before her, dripping wet, holding a white towel around his waist. "Good morning," he crooned. "The wildebeests didn't carry you away during the night I see."

Kelli opened her mouth to speak, but nothing came out. He was absolutely gorgeous standing before her, all fresh from the shower, with bulging biceps and his wet hair slicked back. She simply looked up at him, then down, and then away, her eyes darting all over the place in an attempt to avoid considering that he was standing before her wearing nothing but a flimsy towel around his waist.

He smiled, a quite ravishing smile, exposing those maddeningly white teeth. "The wildebeests may not have carried you off, but some exotic cat must have taken your tongue." He laughed out loud at his own joke.

She stiffened, feeling her face redden and growing furious with his obvious enjoyment of her uneasiness. "I'm glad you are enjoying yourself at my expense. I'll be waiting back in my cabin while you dress," she retorted saucily and then descended his stairs, leaving him half-naked in the doorway still smiling.

A few minutes later he arrived at her cabin, dressed in jeans and a polo shirt. "Hey, I'm sorry if I made you uncomfortable a little while ago," he said in a serious manner, although his mischievous eyes reflected anything but remorse.

"There's no need to apologize, Jace. It was nothing," she answered, although she couldn't meet his eyes quite yet. "We have about 15 minutes until Totseui arrives. Let's see if this place serves breakfast."

Together they walked back over to the office and to their delight, saw that a buffet-style breakfast was being served in a small area off the lobby. They helped themselves to a hot, thick cereal that resembled grits, an assortment of fresh fruit, and some hot tea. At this point, they were so hungry that they probably would have chased down and eaten a live bear. They were sitting at a small corner table when they saw Totseui come in the office door. He spotted them immediately and waved, walking over.

"Would you like to eat with us?" Kelli asked, as she stood to greet him.

"No, I eat already," he answered, rubbing his belly as if in great satisfaction. "I see you eat *nshima*." He nodded toward the thick, hot cereal.

"What is this made from?" asked Jace, hungrily devouring it.

"*Nshima* is porridge made from ground corn. For breakfast, it is sweetened with sugar."

"It's actually delicious. It reminds me of what we call 'grits' back in the states," Kelli said.

"Nshima is staple food," explained Totseui. "Many Zambians eat it two times day. It fill you up, gives lots energy. For dinner, we eat with fish or other meat."

They polished off their tea and then left with Totseui for the 15-minute drive to Kelli's farm. "You hear animal sounds last night?" Totseui asked them.

"I don't know about you, Kelli, but I heard distant howling and lots of chirping insects," offered Jace. Kelli nodded in agreement.

"You probably hear hyenas, leopards and lions. They all roam the prairies east of the rainforest and there are large amounts of them."

"That's a place we plan to visit while we are here," said Jace.

"I'd love to see them in their natural habitat, just not outside my hut during the night," Kelli remarked.

They jounced along on the jutted, dirt road until they came to a much narrower dirt lane that turned to the right. "Here we are," said Totseui, pointing to a fence. "Your farm begins here."

Kelli sat up straight and leaned out the window in an attempt to capture every detail of the cropland. A crudely-built log fence stretched along the back wall of the property. Neat, long rows of glossy green plants, about two feet high, rose above trenches of dark, rich, fertile soil. The rainy season had just ended and the plants looked healthy and lush. There were acres and acres of these rows, all lined up and freshly hoed. About a dozen workers, wearing long-sleeved shirts as a protection from the sun, were continuing to hoe.

Totseui parked the jeep in front of a small, ramshackle shed and got out. "This is both office and storage," he explained. "Farm files, baskets, tools—it is all here."

Before going inside, Kelli asked for a few minutes to walk around. She strolled down the neatly-planted rows, feeling the black loose soil underfoot, stopping to admire the texture and feel of the plants. She had never even see the arabechia plant before and while breathing it and touching it, she felt the powerful connection between man and nature. She realized the cutting-edge research that revolved around this plant and marveled at the potency that lied within its leaves to help cure certain types of cancer.

She walked the rows and shook hands with the workers, men with weathered faces and leathery hands, the result of years of toiling the land. Most could not speak English, but bowed and smiled, their mouths revealing crooked and missing teeth. Clearly, Totseui had informed the workers that she would be here, and they acted as if she were royalty, which greatly touched her heart. She closed her hands around some of the workers' own hands and bowed in return, hoping they would nonverbally understand that she was grateful for their hard work and commitment to this farm. She then walked back to the shed to join Jace and Totseui who had been standing in front of the shed, watching her heartwarming interaction with the workers.

The rest of the day was spent with Totseui showing them around the farm, and then going inside the shed to review files while sitting around an ancient wooden table with layers of flaking paint. They discussed past harvests, future projections, and expansion plans. There was so much to talk about, and the time passed much too quickly.

Totseui took them to a small cafe down the road for dinner where he ordered all of them *amaranthus* soup. "It made from milk, onions, spinach and spices," he explained. They also had *ndiwa* (beans). Kelli noticed that the food, like the people here, was extremely simple and realized that Americans were actually pretty spoiled with all the fancy foods they were accustomed to having for their meals.

* * * * * * * *

The next day was spent pretty much like the previous one, and Kelli and Totseui discussed expanding the farm and adding additional workers from the village, pending the contract between the interested labs once the arabechia was harvested.

"If we can generate enough interest in this herb, and if it meets the expectations of the scientists in the labs, then we may be looking at growing many more plants and hiring many more workers," Kelli mused aloud to Totseui one afternoon.

"The village would be happy," said Totseui. "Men always need work here, and this farm would help more families raise little ones."

Jace sat in on all the discussions and plans, offering suggestions when asked. He had a wonderful medical perspective and a keen, sharp mind, and Kelli relied heavily on his input and wisdom.

On the third day of their visit, Totseui drove them to a manufacturing facility a couple hours away, and there they met with the manager and discussed manufacturing methods and timelines for shipping the harvested herb to the interested labs in a timely manner. They looked at packing arrangements and travel times to ensure the herb's freshness. They also toured the facility and checked out the machines that harvested an array of Zambian crops.

That evening Totseui recommended a restaurant in a nearby small town, and they left for it straight from the manufacturing facility. Kelli felt as if she should at least brush her hair and change to a clean blouse, but Totseui assured her that she looked fine and that it wasn't a place she had to dress up for.

He was right. They entered a large sheet metal building that was decorated inside with huge animal heads from the owner's hunting expeditions. There were large potted palm trees and rustic iron doors that opened onto a large veranda on which sat nearly two dozen metal picnic tables covered in bright red linens. Zambian music spilled from the speakers and the waiters were dressed in puffy, tan-colored shirts which were unbuttoned to the waist. In Kelli's opinion it was just the type of eatery that one envisioned when thinking of an African restaurant.

They followed their waiter outside to a table and sat in the warm air. They ordered cold bottles of water and ate chikanda, which was a dish cooked from tubers, grilled antelope meat, *and delele*. Totseui made the recommendations for their food choices and explained that *delele* refers to various wild greens. "Zambia also has big amount of antelopes," he added. "Many restaurants serve its meat in cooked dishes."

They enjoyed their meal with Totseui immensely and listened as he told stories of his boyhood. He was born and raised in the village where he still resides, but he regaled them with tales of his great-grandpa and great uncles and their ancestors who were tribesman and told of their ceremonial rituals. "You see tribal ceremonies today for visitors," he told them. "You must see one before you leave."

"That sounds wonderful. Tomorrow Jace and I plan to go on safari on one of the great prairies east of here," Kelli interjected.

"You play now," said Totseui, smiling. "Your work done."

"Well, most of the work. I still want to go over some more ideas with you before we leave."

"I be here at farm," affirmed Totseui. Then, looking over at Jace he gave a warning. "If you travel back toward Lusaka, do not walk down Cairo Road, Lumumba Road, and that area after dark. Violent robberies have happened there."

"Thank you, Totseui. We will be picked up tomorrow by a guide who will take us on safari, so we will ride with him."

Kelli insisted on paying for their meals, and then they once again loaded up in Totseui's jeep, and he drove them back to the lodge. It was dark when they returned, and the outdoor lantern lights on each little hut were lit brightly. He bid them good-bye and promised to see them again in a couple days.

Jace and Kelli were enjoying the night air and strolling slowly toward their huts when Jace pointed out a small seating area down by a pond behind the lodge. "Let's sit outside for a moment," he suggested. He reached for Kelli's hand, and they walked down the gentle slope to the outdoor bench which was constructed by resting a slab of native teakwood atop two boulders. He pulled her down beside him on the bench and then wrapped his arm around her shoulders.

"So, what is your impression of Zambia, and in particular, of your farm?" he probed.

Kelli inhaled the sweet, night scent and sighed. "It is a beautiful country, and the natives are very nice, hard-working people. As for my farm, I didn't quite know what to expect, but the actual rows of the herb are neater and more compact than I had imagined. And the shed just resembles an old potting shed in someone's back yard, yet that is where all the daily business is performed." She cocked her head slightly as she spoke. "There seems to be so much potential in the use of this herb, if it all works out." She turned to look at Jace. "What was your impression?"

He was completely lost in watching the play of moonlight on her golden hair and the shadows that her long eyelashes cast along her cheekbones. He didn't hear her question until she called his name.

"Jace?"

He couldn't help himself. He absolutely could not deny himself the carnal pleasure of this moment in an exotic land. Slowly, he leaned over and gently touched her lips with his, savoring their softness, their fullness, their responsiveness. He pulled her closer and deepened the kiss and she responded with just as much zeal and enthusiasm until finally a small moan escaped her throat.

She suddenly pulled away and gasped for breath. "What are we doing, Jace?" she asked, looking genuinely bewildered.

Jace was not ready for the kiss to end. "I think it's obvious what we were doing, Kel," he answered, a roguish look in his eyes. "And if I'm not mistaken, you were enjoying yourself maybe as much as I was."

"Jace, no, we can't," she breathlessly answered, shaking her head furiously. "We can't mess up what we have between us."

"What are you talking about? Mess what up?" He was attempting, but clearly failing, to follow her train of thought.

"Oh, Jace, you've been my friend for about as long as I can remember." She took a deep breath, trying to find a way to explain this in an easier way, but there was none. "I don't want to mess that up."

"Why would we mess up anything?" Jace questioned, obviously not following her reasoning.

"Don't you see? We used to be best friends, and even now we share a strong bond of friendship. Once we cross over that line of friendship . . ." she stopped talking and swallowed hard, trying to make Jace see her point. "Don't you understand? If it didn't work out between us, I don't think I could stand losing our friendship, too. You've been like family to me since we were kids."

Jace was staring at her. "Are you attracted to me, Kelli?" He searched her face in the silvery glow of the moon. "Or am I simply like a brother or some other family member to you?"

"Oh, Jace." Her mind shot back to a of couple days before and conjured up the image of him standing in the doorway wearing nothing but a towel, and the fiery reaction it had caused in the pit of her belly. "I am so very attracted to you. What woman wouldn't be? I mean, look at you— you look like a Greek god—and you have a spectacular body, and to top it off, you are a cardiologist." She was wringing her hands in agitation. "I mean, it's strange because I can remember you being my best friend when we were little, and now . . . here you are, and I still feel like you are my friend, but you've changed from the little boy I remember to this desirable hunk, and I don't know quite how I'm supposed to feel around you anymore."

Jace was softly laughing at her. He pulled her against his strong chest again, running his fingers through her hair. "How about if we don't try too hard at remembering what we used to be and instead focus on whom we are now, and what we feel today?"

He nuzzled her hair with his cheek. "I know one thing, Kel. I find you extremely desirable, and the fact that we have been friends for so long only strengthens my feelings for you." He kissed her again, gently this time. "However, I will honor your wishes and take as long as you want. You just let me know when you are ready to cross that line." He wiggled his eyebrows at her, then stood and reached for her hand. "Are you ready to call it a night? We have a big safari adventure awaiting us in the morning."

She smiled as he pulled her up, and they walked back to their huts, holding hands. Kelli was grateful for Jace's understanding and patience and hoped he didn't think she was being juvenile. She was convinced that fate had led them to live across from one another again, giving them a second chance at sharing one another's life for whatever reason.

She was also convinced that in the innermost secret pocket of her heart, she was helplessly falling deeply in love with this man.

Chapter 13

The soft light of early dawn lent a pink shimmer to the African landscape, partly due to rising mist from the nearby rain forest. All the now-familiar night sounds had ceased, and in their place came wake-up calls from native birds such as the green barbet and the fire finch.

Kelli was standing at the open window of her hut, having awakened from an unsettling dream. In it, she and Jace were kids again and were playing hide and seek in her back yard. Kelli was "it" and was standing against a tree with her eyes closed, counting to 100. When she opened her eyes, the little ghost girl from her childhood was standing before her, beckoning her closer, while mouthing the words *find Jace.*

After awaking from the dream, Kelli couldn't fall back asleep, so she'd gotten out of bed and watched the dawn of a new day in this extraordinary and beautiful foreign country. She wondered if Jace were up yet, but figured that he was probably still in a deep slumber. She showered and dressed in a cotton blouse and khaki shorts, then pulled her hair back into a ponytail since the majority of the day would be spent riding in a jeep on safari.

In the next hut, Jace had been lying wide awake since the wee hours of the morning. He had replayed the conversation from the night before over and over in his head. For the life of him, he couldn't understand how Kelli thought that he could ever abandon her and reject the friendship they had forged almost two decades earlier. Sure, taking things to the next level could complicate their life in some ways if it didn't work out, but he would never think about ending their friendship. He decided to just leave the timing to Kelli and pray that she would come to her senses sooner, rather than later. Women tended to be funny about things like that, feeling the need to sort their emotions in an orderly fashion before proceeding with a relationship. Men just went with the flow.

He grimaced, before finally deciding to get up and get dressed. He was looking forward to a true, authentic African safari. And he had to admit that he was also eagerly anticipating spending the day with Kelli.

As Kelli came bounding down the steps of her hut, she saw Jace coming out of his hut at the same time. She waved, and he cheerily returned the wave, and they walked together to the lobby for breakfast. She was thankful that he seemed to act perfectly normal around her, despite the subject matter of their little talk the night before.

Once inside, Jace picked up a colorful ceramic bowl and heaped a thick spoonful of *nshima* in it.

"Yum," he wisecracked. "I'm going to miss this stuff for breakfast every morning when we return home."

Kelli grinned. "Even plain oatmeal is actually starting to sound very appealing to me again," she admitted.

While they ate they discussed all the sights and animals that they hoped to encounter on the safari. As soon as they had finished with breakfast, the safari driver arrived and after talking with the front deskman, walked over to greet them. He was a tall, huskily-built dark man and wore a tan shirt with matching shorts. He shook their hands and spoke fluent English as he introduced himself as Saulcho. Dressed as he was and with binoculars hanging from his neck and a straw hat perched atop his head, Kelli thought he fit the image of a safari guide perfectly.

They chatted a few minutes and then he escorted them to a 1970's style 4-wheel drive bronco that had its roof removed and the name "Zambia Safari Adventures" painted on the door. In the back, comfortable chairs were aligned in a "U" shape and a rollover bar hung overhead that they could grab onto when crossing rough terrain.

They headed east following a decently-paved road then turned west, toward the plains on the outskirts of the Zambezi River basin where the road turned to gravel and was pitted with the now-predictable potholes.

Keeping one hand on the steering wheel, Saulcho pointed to his right with his other hand, making a sweeping gesture. "This area is all part of the Zambezi River basin. The Zambezi River is the fourth largest river in Africa and the largest flowing into the Indian Ocean from Africa."

Soon they arrived at an entrance to a vast prairie. "We are here at last," Saulcho announced, gearing the bronco down into second, as he pulled onto the grassy terrain. The trail ahead, which was nothing more than a dirt path, resembled a forgotten, ancient road and was probably created solely by the tires of vehicles bringing visitors on safari expeditions.

For the next few hours they rode over the rugged land, standing in the back holding onto the overhead bar, reveling in the African landscape that was so foreign to them. They drove right beside a herd of zebras, grazing in the meadow, and later saw elephants walking toward a watering hole near a bamboo grove. Saulcho passed his binoculars back to Kelli and Jace and pointed out a lion perched on a rocky overhang quite a distance from them, but nonetheless watching the trio intently. As they came upon a small stream of water, they saw Nile crocodiles basking on a sandbar. A little further away, rhinos were grazing in an open field.

"In a few remote areas, there are still black rhinos," Saulcho informed them. "However, they were largely destroyed by poachers in the 1970's and 1980's."

"What a shame," Kelli remarked sadly.

Around noon Saulcho parked the bronco beneath the shade of an acacia tree and the three of them drank bottled water and ate ripe plantains and papayas which he provided. The whole expedition was one of unparalleled beauty and learning. To be in the natural setting of creatures that Americans usually only see in zoos, was very exhilarating to both Jace and Kelli.

They completed the safari experience with another member of the safari guide team taking a picture of the three of them standing together, arm-in-arm, smiling. Jace and Kelli had each taken countless pictures during the expedition as well.

That evening they ate dinner back at the lodge while they laughed and relived the entire day. Their faces looked sun-kissed and they were exhausted, but in a good way, and the next day they were going to meet with Totseui for a final time before they departed Zambia in two days. As they exited the lodge, they took a few minutes to walk down to the bench near the water and take advantage of the beautiful night, lit by an exquisitely bright, full moon.

Jace reached over for Kelli's hand as soon as they sat down. "Thanks again for inviting me to accompany you here, Kel. I couldn't think of anyone else I would want to share all these experiences with."

Kelli noticed that the golden light from the moon caused his grey eyes to shoot flecks of fire and the night's shadows only helped to define the muscular jawline of his rugged face. She had the sudden longing to reach out and touch his cheeks, to run her finger along his lips. Instead, she simply sat frozen in place, staring at the handsome man who had traveled halfway around the world with her, and at this moment she recognized that she trusted him with her whole heart.

A lot of this realization was due to the fact that their tight bond of friendship had never disappeared. Although they had been apart for nearly two decades, their bond of friendship was still solid and tight. What they shared was a lasting bond, one that couldn't be broken by time, nor changed by distance.

Yet now a different kind of relationship, one which included romantic feelings, had taken root and begun to grow. It was not replacing their original bond, but simply enhancing it, for the foundation of their friendship would always be traced back to their youth and would never, ever disintegrate, not in a thousand years.

A smile formed on Kelli's lips as her mind grasped this truth. She squeezed Jace's hand as she answered his earlier comment. "I know, because I feel exactly the same way. Thank you for taking time off from your busy schedule and coming here with me. I felt much more confident at the farm meetings knowing you were at the table with me. I highly value your intelligence," she said, playfully tapping his head with her fingertips.

He reached up and caught her hand with his and held it. The moonlight spotlighted them in its ethereal glow as they sat together on the log bench near the brackish water. Jace slowly leaned down and kissed her with such tenderness that it caused her breath to catch. He then pulled her against his chest and with his strong arms encircling her, held her close. Kelli closed her eyes and found herself wishing that they could stay this way forever.

* * * * * *

Kelli was deep asleep, lost in some kind of wild African dream. In it she was sitting with other tribal people around an open fire at night, and there was a lot of dancing and chanting and crude, ancient-looking instruments that drummed out ancestral songs. The rhythmic chanting grew louder and more intense as Kelli struggled to wake up, her mind wandering in a thick fog. The dream had seemed so very real.

She slowly opened her eyes to see flickering firelight casting shadows on the inside walls of her hut. Funny, she could still hear the pounding of drums and the collective chants of the tribesmen from her dream.

Something was not right with this scene, she thought, sitting up groggily and trying to fight her way out of the fog. Suddenly, her body became taut; her senses on full alert as she realized that the chanting was not lingering from her dream but was coming from outside her hut at that very moment.

Kelli quickly jumped out of bed and walked toward the open window, only to realize that she would be visible to all who were out there since there was no window covering. She dropped down and crept to the side of the window, then inched upward until she could barely peek out of the bottom edge. She gulped as she observed the scene in front of her.

In the darkness that was illuminated by a full moon, stood a group of men wearing animal loin cloths around their waists. There appeared to be twelve, maybe fifteen men, and they were holding barbaric lanterns made from sticks and fire. Some wore the heads of dead animals and carried spears, whose tips appeared reddened, no doubt from dried blood. They had stripes painted on their upper arms and their faces were darkened, probably with either paint or mud. A few wore elaborate, feathered headdresses, and they all were participating in a tribal chant, their voices rising, then falling, and then rising to a crescendo while simultaneously jabbing the sticks of flaming fire high above their heads. They repeated this chant, along with the tribal dance, over and over, each time moving a bit closer to Kelli and Jace's huts.

Kelli tried her best not to panic, but to maintain control. What was she going to do? She couldn't even speak their language to attempt to communicate with them. Her first thought was of Jace, and how she wished he were standing beside her at this very moment. He may not know how to communicate with them either, but he always seemed to know what to do in any situation, and she would feel safer knowing he was with her. She suddenly felt frightfully alone in a foreign country and realized that she probably would have felt this way often during the entire trip, had Jace not accompanied her.

Thinking of Jace, she wondered if the chants had awakened him yet, and if he was aware of the situation outside. There was no way to contact him, no phone service, no internet access, nothing. She inched her way along the wall to the window again and tried to see if Jace were at his window. His hut was about 50 feet from hers and with his window adjacent to hers, she would have to hang out and shout at him to talk, something she certainly did not want to attempt, given the current situation. She stood straight and flat against the wall and leaned her head back, listening to the eerie chants growing disturbingly closer. The chanting certainly didn't sound celebratory, but angry—even hostile.

Suddenly, she heard her name being called loudly and recognized Jace's voice amid the racket. She took a deep breath to gather her courage and then hung out her window as far as she felt comfortable and saw Jace doing the same outside of his window, wildly waving in her direction.

"I'm coming over to your hut, Kelli," he yelled through cupped hands.

"Jace, no!" Kellie shouted back. "It's too dangerous. You don't know what these men may do to you!"

"I'm coming, anyway!" Jace yelled in answer. "Have your door ready to open when I reach the top step."

He immediately retreated back inside his hut. The men had witnessed the exchange between the two of them and were widening their circle around the huts, their chanting becoming increasingly louder, as if in proportion to their mounting fury.

Kelli ran to her door, ready to open it whenever she heard Jace's footsteps outside on the stairs. She stood behind the door waiting for what seemed like an eternity before she summoned up enough nerve to open it and see what was taking Jace so much time.

She let out a shriek when she saw Jace standing between their two huts, completely encircled by the tribesmen, waving their flickering fire lanterns above their heads, their chants obviously not friendly. Jace appeared to be completely calm as he held his hands up in front of him in an attempt to signify peace.

116

Kelli couldn't let him handle this alone. She hurried down the steps, not knowing what to do, her heart thudding wildly in her chest. Just then she heard a man shouting and she turned to see the lodge's night manager, Answai, approaching the group. He was also trying to communicate with the group by smiling and bowing while he walked toward them with his palms open.

"Totseui comes," he announced in a loud voice for the benefit of Jace and Kelli, whose faces registered relief upon hearing this news. Kelli was surprised that Answai could speak this much English and hoped they could hold on long enough for Totseui to arrive. The angry chants of the tribesmen were aimed at Jace, but some were separating and heading toward Kelli after seeing her come outside.

For what seemed like hours, Kelli and Jace stayed where they were, trying to convey peace and not making any sudden moves. Suddenly, headlights beamed over the scene as Totseui's jeep came screeching to an abrupt halt, and he jumped out. Kelli felt such relief as she watched her beloved farm manager approach the tribesmen and begin speaking in a foreign language, while waving his hands and gesturing for their torches to be lowered.

All chanting ceased as the men gathered around Totseui, as if curious as to who he was and what he had to say. Jace took this opportunity to move toward Kelli, and she stretched out her arms to him.

The tribesmen stood solemnly while watching Totseui with piercing eyes. Kelli could not make out a word he was saying, but his voice was mesmerizing as it rose with enthusiasm and then lowered peacefully. He was having a difficult time as he couldn't speak their tongue, yet nonetheless, he was communicating with them.

After a while, the tribesmen began lowering their torches of fire and backing away. Whatever Totseui had attempted to say to them had worked, and Kelli knew that she and Jace owed him immeasurably. As the group disappeared back into the dense, dark jungles from which they came, Totseui joined Kelli and Jace.

Kelli was the first to embrace him. "Oh, Totseui, what would we have done without you? What did they want?"

Totseui explained that word had traveled to them about a couple of white men arriving, and the rumor was that white men would steal jobs and food from the natives. "I explained to them that you *give* jobs to locals, not take them away and you want to help provide more jobs."

Jace appeared concerned. "What tribe are they from?"

"They are cast-offs from old, old Ngoni tribe. This tribe adopted fighting tactics of Great Shaka Zula. They live by old ways of long ago." Totseui paused, while thinking. "Today, there is little tribal animosity in Zambia, which good."

Jace and Kelli hugged Totseui again and thanked him profusely. He returned their embrace, coupled with a smile, and seemed genuinely pleased to help them with this frightening ordeal.

Jace glanced at his watch, noting aloud that it was close to three in the morning. "We'll see you again in about five hours for breakfast, Totseui. Maybe you can get some more sleep."

Totseui bowed and wished the same to them.

After he left, Kelli turned to Jace with a serious expression.

"I'll be the first to admit that I was terrified, Jace." She went to him with open arms and laid her head on his chest. "What would I have done, had I been here alone?"

"Don't even dwell on that thought, Kelli. It wasn't going to happen tonight, nor will it happen in the future, because I will always be here for you, if you need me."

He wrapped his arms around her slender waist. "You're shaking like a leaf. Let's get you inside." He gently led her up the stairs of her hut, opened the door and stood aside for her to enter.

Kelli stepped inside and motioned for Jace to follow. She closed the door behind him and turned to him, her eyes boldly locked on his.

"Don't leave me tonight."

His eyes followed her gaze as it leisurely traveled over the rugged contours of his face. In her impassioned eyes he could read the incredibly seductive, yet highly combustible, mix of fear and desire.

"Please. Stay with me."

This was no child talking to him after awaking from a bad dream. Although what they had just experienced had been truly frightening, her eyes revealed a set of entirely different feelings. His overwhelming compulsion to be with her overshadowed the danger he knew lurked by his staying.

Jace took a step closer to Kelli, and cautiously reached for her, all the while searching her face for any possible reluctance. There was none.

She made the first move by closing her eyes and tilting her face up toward his. He was quite capable of taking it from there, as he swept her into his strong arms and hungrily kissed her lips. His mind was telling him to slow down, but all of his pent-up passion was spilling out, and it was as impossible to contain as it was to command the ocean to cease its waves.

"Kelli," he whispered, "we don't have to do anything you will regret; I promise."

He tightened his arms around her, feeling compelled to protect her with his whole being, not just tonight, but forever, until the end of time. This friend, this girl who had grown to become such an amazing woman and who had been such an integral part of his childhood, was back in his life again for a reason. Destiny had brought her back for a purpose he suddenly knew, as he squeezed her tighter and nuzzled her hair, inhaling the intoxicating scent that was hers alone.

"I won't regret anything, Jace. I want this more than I've ever wanted anything in my life before."

His head was spinning, his heart was pounding, and his emotions were whirling like a dizzying carnival ride. He knew without a doubt that he loved this woman with every fiber of his being. In his heart of hearts, he had no question.

Chapter 14

The high-pitched calling of a flock of fire finches in the nearby miombo forest caused Kelli's eyelids to slowly flutter open. For a few seconds her grogginess created murkiness in her memory as flashbacks of tribal dancing and spears flashed across her mind.

But there was something more, something of supreme importance that had occurred. As she became fully awake, she realized what it was. Jace was sleeping soundly beside her, his arm protectively draped across her waist.

In an instant, the previous night's events came flooding back to her. Jace had come to her rescue. He had risked his life to come to her hut and save her. Who knows what those crazy tribal men could have done to him before Totseui arrived?

Not only that, he had stayed the remainder of the night with her, after she was so frightened and too scared to be alone. At that moment, she had known that Jace would always protect her, if she let him. When they were children he had rescued her from bike accidents and imaginary bad guys. Now, he was still rescuing her—this time from frightening tribal men in a foreign land. Except this encounter had not been imaginary, but all too real.

Her instinct had told her that she could always depend on him. Was she wrong to do so? Was their current relationship simply shaped by memories of a childhood friendship? Regardless of the reason, she had known without question last night that she could count on him. She knew that Jace would be there to save her, protect her, comfort her. She had fallen asleep in his arms, feeling completely safe from whatever danger might still loom outside the hut.

Kelli could hear his soft breathing beside her. Slowly, she eased out of bed and into the tiny bathroom. After a long, steamy shower, she emerged wrapped in a towel to find Jace sitting against the headboard, the pillows propped up behind him. His disheveled hair, day-old stubble and full lips which curved into a slow smile caused heat to stir deep in her belly.

It should be illegal for any man to look that good.

"You look a lot calmer this morning than you did a few hours ago," Jace said, while patting the side of the bed in invitation for her to come over.

Kelli walked over and perched on the bed's edge. "Those guys were so creepy in the flickering firelight, doing all that strange dancing and chanting. It was like we had stepped back in time and landed in the middle of some angry tribal ritual."

Jace considered this. "In a sense, we did. Those men were throwbacks from a tribe centuries ago. Even though the world has progressed, they haven't. Much of their life today is lived the same way as their ancestors lived hundreds of years ago."

He brushed a wet strand of hair from her forehead. "As they saw it, you and I were a threat to their culture by possibly taking away some of their land. Thankfully, Totseui showed up when he did and attempted to explain that we were not their enemies. At least, I hope that was the impression they got."

"Me, too. Speaking of Totseui, we have to meet him for breakfast shortly and say our goodbyes." Kelli paused, looking somewhat embarrassed. "About last night," she began.

"Yeah? Which part are you referring to?" Jace playfully prodded.

"You know which part. I was just so frightened and really needed someone to stay with me."

"Someone? You mean that just anyone would have been suitable?" teased Jace.

Kelli blushed. "You're making this really difficult, Jace."

"Oh am I?" he leaned forward and kissed her earlobe, as he pulled her down beside him, and together they slid under the sheets.

* * * * * * *

A while later Jace and Kelli sat with Totseui in the lobby's dining area for one last breakfast together before their departure. After discussing the scare with the tribesmen from the night before, Kelli and Jace again thanked him for his timely arrival and handling the situation for them.

Totseui had a few more papers for Kelli to sign, and they discussed the farm's operations and future expansion one last time in person.

"After today our conversations will again have to be done over the phone," Kelli said to Totseui. "It was such a pleasure to meet you face-to-face. You are a very special person to me, and after today I am confident that my farm is in good hands with you as the manager."

Totseui flashed a meek grin and appeared embarrassed for being in the spotlight.

After breakfast they checked out of the lodge, and Totseui drove them in his old jeep down the bumpy, dirt roads on the long journey back to the airport where they exchanged goodbyes and hugs one last time.

When Jace and Kelli were alone waiting in the airport lobby to board the first of many flights to return home, Jace turned to Kelli. "Are you going to miss this place?"

"I'll miss Totseui, my farm, the romance of the country, the splendor of the jungles and safari," she replied, tilting her head in thought. "But, I'm ready to return home again." She caught herself. "Listen to me, I'm already referring to my little house as home," she laughed.

"It *is* your home. You spent many years there as a child. Just because you moved away to another state for years doesn't change how your heart feels. Once you've lived in a house, your essence is forever imprinted on it." As soon as he said the words, he and Kelli stared at each other.

"Do you think the ghost girl was an imprint on the house from someone who once lived there?" Kelli cautiously asked.

"Perhaps," Jace said, as he considered this possibility. "Something has tied her to the house, and yeah, I guess that's her imprint on the place. Maybe her spirit happens to be her imprint, I don't know."

It was announced that their small plane was fueled, checked, and now cleared to board.

"I do know one thing, Kelli," Jace said, as he picked up their carry-on bags and headed out toward the plane. "I am going to help you get to the bottom of this."

* * * * * * * *

It was a perfect day for flying as their plane smoothly glided through scattered, cottony clouds. Down below, gorgeous African plains consisting of vivid colors that ranged from copper to gold and green, meshed with thick dark jungles that housed all types of monkeys and reptiles and who knew what else. A large herd of elephants, barely visible from high in the air, moved about the plains.

Zambia was a beautiful country, one full of exotic animals, hard-working, friendly people, and ancient customs, and Kelli knew that this trip was one that she would make again in the future, if she kept her farm. The plane was scheduled to follow the same route as before, stopping in Rome, and then making the lengthy trek back across the Atlantic to New York.

A flight attendant passed out blankets and pillows for the passengers to sleep as they prepared to make the long flight over the ocean. Jace snuggled down in his seat toward Kelli, and she rested her head on his shoulder. At one point, he woke up and looked down at Kelli who was still asleep on his shoulder, and the sight warmed his heart and made him smile. He was surprised at how natural it felt to have her there, and how much closer this trip had brought them together.

He watched her shoulders slowly move up and down as she breathed, and he knew in his heart that he loved her, truly and deeply. He remembered having a brief crush on her at some point in their childhood, but this feeling he was now experiencing was no crush, but something that he was sure would endure for a lifetime and even beyond.

By the time they passed through all of the time changes, it was early evening the next day when they pulled into Kelli's driveway. A warm feeling washed over Kelli as soon as she saw her pretty little house, looking spruced up with its exterior scrubbed and the overgrown shrubs whipped back in shape. Its appearance was a far cry from the first time she had seen it a few months ago.

From her kitchen window, Mrs. Tanner had seen them pull into the driveway and came hurrying over.

"Welcome home! I've been watching for you two," she gushed, as she gave Kelli and then Jace a tight hug. "It just hasn't been the same around here knowing you both were gone." She put her hands on Kelli's shoulders and looked her squarely in the eye. "Kelli, even though you have just moved back home, it already doesn't feel right whenever you are not here."

Kelli planted a quick kiss on Mrs. Tanner's cheek. "Thank you. You know, it just feels right to be here. I'm so glad to be back."

Jace was unloading her bags from the trunk and carrying them to the front door. Kelli fished around for her house keys while Mrs. Tanner invited them to dinner the next night. "I know you two are absolutely bushed tonight from your long trip, but I can't wait to hear about it and thought you could tell me everything over a home-cooked meal tomorrow night."

Kelli looked at Jace, who nodded eagerly. "Sounds wonderful to me. I'm ready for some good home-cooked American food consisting of anything but *nshima.*"

Kelli laughed in agreement and explained to Mrs. Tanner that *nshima* was a staple in Zambia that was present in various forms for most meals.

Mrs. Tanner shook her head. "Doesn't sound all that appetizing to me. Dinner tomorrow night should be a cinch to fix because anything I serve should be a hit to two weary travelers who are starved for American food."

As Kelli and Jace smiled at her comment, she couldn't help but notice that there was something different between the two of them.

Jace sat Kelli's luggage inside the door for her and then kissed her on the cheek and muttered, "Get some sleep. I'll talk to you in the morning."

He seemed as exhausted as she did. She locked the door behind him then checked each room of her house, before taking a hot shower. She fell into bed, deciding to wait and unpack her suitcases the next day. Jet lag was really hard on a person she realized, as she sunk into the comfort of her own bed, and her eyes closed immediately.

* * * * * * * *

Kelli awakened to the sound of a chirping bird, and for a minute she thought that she was still in Zambia, listening to the familiar chirping of the African fire finch calling from the jungles. She looked around her room, half expecting to see the furnishings of the hut, but slowly realized that she was back in Arkansas, and the chirping bird was nothing more than a common mockingbird sitting on the holly bush outside her window. She looked at the clock and was surprised to discover that she had slept for a solid twelve hours and couldn't remember when she had last slept that long.

She pulled the covers back and climbed out of bed, eager to fall back into a routine and catch up on all that needed to be done around the house. She also needed to begin all the follow-up work concerning her farm. She walked to the kitchen, spooned coffee grounds into the coffeemaker basket, added water, and then walked to the window overlooking the backyard while she waited for the coffee to perk.

The eastern sky was just beginning to lighten, igniting the neighborhood in a golden hue. It felt good to be back, she thought, and then wondered how Jace was adjusting. She glanced out the back window toward his house and gasped at the sight beyond it.

On the hillside above his house loomed a majestic structure that had been completely framed since their departure. It resembled a forest of 2x4's. Make that a three-story forest. The thing looked like a castle, she thought. Whatever was Jace thinking when he decided to build such a place? She poured herself a cup of coffee and decided to rib him a little whenever she saw him that day, which happened to be sooner rather than

127

later, because Jace walked over a couple hours later while Kelli was unpacking and doing her laundry from the trip.

She answered his knock, and he swooped down with a big embrace, followed by a kiss.

"It seemed strange to sleep alone last night after spending the previous two nights with you." At Kelli's questioning look, he explained. "Remember, the night before we were together on the plane all night, and the night before that was when I stayed with you in your hut after the tribal incident."

He had a small smirk on his face, and his eyebrows shot up at the memory of that night. "So, I was lonely last night."

Kelli returned his kiss. "If you're lonely now, you are really going to be lonely in about a year from now."

He pulled back, frowning, and looked in Kelli's eyes. "What's that supposed to mean?"

"It means that the monstrosity of a house you are having constructed is going to have so many rooms in it that you could fill it with 200 people and still be lonely."

Laughing at her exaggeration, Jace grasped her hands. "The builders have really done a lot since we left. The framing is almost completely finished, and next they will roof it."

He looked as if an idea suddenly occurred to him. "Hey, let's go see it right now." Remembering his manners, he quickly added, "That is, if you are not in the middle of doing something."

"Just laundry," she droned, "which I'm sure you have a lot of, as well."

"Oh, right, the laundry. I guess I'll need to get started on that soon." He smiled, and in her mind she could see the impish face and playful eyes of him as a boy attempting to shirk his chores. "Or, I could just send it all to the cleaners to have it done."

"No fair," Kelli complained. "If I have to do trip laundry, then you have to do trip laundry." She already felt good and rested, even a bit spirited this morning.

"Yes, dear, if you insist," he said in a whiny voice. Jace was in a happy, teasing mood as well. The trip had done them both good. "Now, get your sneakers on and let's go."

Soon they had crossed the road and were climbing the pasture toward the rolling hillside above Jace's current home. As they climbed higher, the enormity of the house stretched before them.

"It does appear somewhat large," Jace surmised, his gaze sweeping the massive framed structure. "However, I think that once it's bricked and enclosed, it will look different."

"Probably even larger," Kelli refuted, under her breath.

Jace led the way to the front entrance and then stepped aside for her to enter. "This will be the entry foyer and to the left will be the living room," he explained. "There will be a two-story stone fireplace here. I want it made using native rocks from the top of this hillside."

Kelli raised her eyebrows. "You mean from the Enemy Lookout Tower area?" she asked.

"That's the very spot," Jace answered, pleased that she remembered the cowboy and Indian game she was referring to that they had so often played there.

Kelli walked to the middle of the floor and looked out over the neighborhood where so many of her prized childhood memories were formed. Below, looped the narrow paved road, which used to be gravel, where she rode her bike each day. To her left was the small glistening pond where many summer afternoons were spent fishing, and to the right sat the old red barn, its paint now mostly flaked off, where they used to climb in the hay. Across the road sat her beloved little house, looking well-tended and loved once more. In recent years newer homes had been built, and businesses had sprung up further down the road, but in her mind's eye she saw the area as it appeared over twenty years ago. Jace's new house was being built high on a hillside providing a spectacular view of the Fayetteville skyline, framed by the lush, dense Ozark Mountains beyond.

Jace fell silent as he watched her slowly spin around in an attempt to capture and savor the priceless view that was spread before her. It was a moving moment for him as he drank in the sight of Kelli, who was oblivious to him watching her and lost in her own world, experiencing long-forgotten memories and feelings that seemed to surface as her eyes scanned the old neighborhood.

He thought he understood pretty much what she was thinking and feeling because this spot was significant to him, too. This location was a vital part of their past and helped to create and shape who they each had become. As he quietly watched her, he wondered who else, but Kelli, would ever be able to experience and share these feelings with him?

He observed her for a moment more, and then slowly walked over and took her hand in his own. Another minute passed as she came out of her reverie and looked into the shimmery depths of his penetrating eyes. They held such tenderness and compassion, but there was something else visibly shining in them that she couldn't quite identify.

He gently pulled her into his arms and kissed her with an intoxicating mix of warmth, understanding and passion. The electricity of his kiss left her breathless and as she looked up into his face, she had no doubt that he was her kindred spirit.

He led her through the maze of frames on the first floor where the den, living room, dining room, kitchen, laundry room and sunroom would be located. They climbed the crudely-built, temporary stairs to the second floor where there would be bedrooms, bathrooms, and a library. The third floor would be divided into a home office for Jace and a room that would be mostly encased in glass to capture the remarkable view. "I want to be able to sit up here and feel like I'm in a tree house," Jace explained.

"I know!" Kelli excitedly suggested. "This room can be known as 'The Enemy Lookout Tower Room!'"

A grin exploded on Jace's face. "Perfect!" he agreed.

They slowly made their way back down the two staircases to the main floor, and Kelli noticed that Jace had grown more quiet and withdrawn. "Kelli," he began, "I don't know much about choosing flooring and paint colors and all that, and since you just finished a beautiful remodeling job, I was wondering if you would be willing to help me with the selections."

Kelli looked at him. "I'd love to, Jace, but you'll have to give me some suggestions on your color and style preferences. I wouldn't want to decorate it in a way that you wouldn't like."

He turned away, carefully inspecting the wooden frames that surrounded them as if he had never seen a 2x4 before in his life, and waited for a long moment before he spoke. "Just choose things that you would want if you were to live in this house."

He turned back to her then with piercing eyes that bore into hers. "If things go as I hope, you will be spending a lot of time here with me."

She didn't know if Jace heard her sharp intake of breath as she nodded her head. "Sure. I'll be glad to do what I can to help," she offered.

Chapter 15

Mrs. Tanner's oblong, oak dining table was spread with an enticing assortment of food. She'd prepared a succulent roast, cooked with carrots and potatoes, homemade rolls, and a fresh lettuce salad. Jace and Kelli's faces lit up when they saw the home-cooked meal and the beautifully set table.

"Kelli, look!" Jace said excitedly, pointing to the table. "It's real food, not *nshima,* or rice, or fruits from the jungle, but REAL food." He draped an arm around Mrs. Tanner's shoulders, pulling her closer. "There is nothing any nicer that anybody could do for me right now, than this." He kissed her cheek, and she playfully slapped his chest.

After they were seated around the table and Jace had offered the blessing, Mrs. Tanner spoke while passing the roast to Kelli. "You two youngsters don't know how much I missed you while you were gone. It was just a lonely little neighborhood without you both. Even though, Jace, you are gone sometimes twelve or more hours a day with your job, I know that you are always here if I need you and it is comforting knowing that you are sleeping across the road at night. Likewise, Kelli, it is so wonderful to have you living next door again." She took a roll and put it on her plate before passing the basket to her. "Now, I want to hear all about the trip, starting with your farm, Kelli."

Kelli began at the beginning, telling her about the numerous flights they endured before finally landing in Zambia and meeting Totseui for the first time. Jace shared in the stories of riding in Totseui's jeep, traveling the primitive, pothole-filled dirt roads, and experiencing Kelli's farm with her.

"Our time there proved to be very productive," said Kelli, while buttering a roll. "We toured a nearby manufacturing facility and met with its manager who expressed a strong interest in doing business with us. We also made plans to enlarge the size of our arabechia crop to meet potential future demand."

"That is wonderful," Mrs. Tanner said while passing the bowl of potatoes around for the second time. "We may soon have quite an important business entrepreneur living amongst us, Jace," she added with a wink.

"What else did you two experience while there? Did you have time for any sightseeing?" As soon as the words were out of her mouth, she could actually almost see the sparks that seemed to fire between Jace and Kelli, and she could practically feel their shared electricity.

They regaled her with tales of the safari adventure, the night calls of the jungle animals, and the loud songs of the land's native birds. They described the lodge's huts and finished with telling her about the unnerving visit during the middle of their last night there from authentic tribesmen. Mrs. Tanner had been leaning forward, intently listening to everything they said, but when they got to this part, her eyes grew wide.

"Do you mean that these tribesmen were REAL? They were chanting and dancing and carrying fire? I'd be terrified! What on earth did you do?"

Kelli answered first. "The lodge manager saw what was occurring, and he called Totseui who arrived shortly thereafter. But we didn't know that, and so Jace came to my rescue." She looked at Jace, and Mrs. Tanner could see the admiration for him shining brightly in Kelli's eyes. "He actually left his hut, surely aware of the danger lurking outside, and was headed to my hut. When he climbed down his steps, the tribesmen all surrounded him, holding their flaming torches above their heads. Then Totseui showed up, and he spoke a little of their language and explained that we were there to help provide jobs, not steal them. Despite his feeble communication with them, they evidently grasped what he was saying and left in peace."

Kelli had finished the story, but her eyes were still intently locked on Jace's as they sat across the table from one another, staring at each other while remembering that night. Mrs. Tanner watched them quietly, looking back and forth from Kelli to Jace, feeling as if she were prying on an intimate moment. Yes, she thought to herself, something had definitely happened between them while they were gone. Something happy and wonderful. Just thinking about this gave her great pleasure.

Later, Kelli and Jace helped Mrs. Tanner clear the table and load the dishwasher. They were again feeling the effects of jet lag and having to readjust their bodies to a different time zone, and so they thanked Mrs. Tanner and kissed her goodnight before it got much later. Jace was scheduled to return to work early the next morning, but insisted on walking Kelli home first.

Once inside her house and seated on her couch, he wrapped his arm around her shoulders and pulled her close. "In all seriousness, I want to thank you for thinking enough of me to want me to travel with you to Zambia. It was an honor, and I thoroughly enjoyed the chance to visit an African country for the first time with you."

Kelli turned toward him and looked up at his profile as he was talking. His nose had a slight bump below the bridge which lent a rugged, manly quality to his face. His piercing grey eyes searched the depths of hers and lingered there for a long moment. "I've also thought a lot about what you told me a few nights ago as we sat outside the lodge. You said that you didn't want to chance losing our friendship by becoming more than friends; that if it didn't work out, we wouldn't be able to go back to the friendship that we've always shared."

He hesitated for a long while, as if trying to choose the right words. "I want you to know, Kelli, that your wish is not possible for me anymore."

Kelli felt her breath catch in her throat, dreading hearing the words that would come from his mouth next. He was preparing to tell her that they could no longer see each other. She knew it. This was all because of the fact that she had asked him to stay the rest of the night with her in the hut on that final night. It was all her fault. They had crossed the line, and now he regretted it.

She silently and harshly reprimanded herself for being surprised. After all, she was the one who put the brakes on any possible future with him for the exact reason that he was now about to explain to her. So, why did she care? Why was her heart beating wildly in her chest, afraid that he might be trying to tell her that their relationship was over before it really even began?

Jace's gaze now returned to Kelli. "It is not possible," he continued, "because I have already crossed the line that you talked about that night. You are not simply a friend from my past, although I treasure that strong bond that forged our relationship many years ago. And perhaps it is because of our history that my feelings for you have intensified. But even more than that, I admire you for the woman you are today and the woman that I know you will always be. I admire your intelligence, your compassion for other human beings, and your values."

He let out a small laugh. "And, obviously I am attracted to you. There is chemistry between us that is very rare. Do you feel it, too, Kelli?"

Kelli was only able to nod her head back and forth while staring into his captivating eyes. "Yes, Jace, I do," she finally managed to utter before his lips found hers. Wrapped in his strong arms and savoring his gentle kisses, she knew at that moment, without a doubt, that she had made the right choice to return to Arkansas. Fate had worked its magic by allowing her to buy her old home on a whim and return only to find that her best childhood buddy had grown into a ruggedly handsome man who still lived across the road. It was as if the pieces of a giant puzzle were suddenly beginning to fit together.

Jace rested his forehead against hers. "All I am sure of right now, Kelli, is that I love you."

Kelli felt her heart literally skip a beat when he said this. "I love you, too, Jace. I suppose I found myself falling in love with you soon after I returned, but subconsciously denied it because I didn't want to mess up our friendship."

"Nothing is messed up, it is only clearer now." Jace pulled back and looked Kelli squarely in the eyes. "I don't know what is going to happen between us or how we plan to handle this gift that has been offered us, but I do know that we were meant to find each other again. Let's just accept that fact and follow our hearts. Whatever is meant to happen will happen."

Jace stood up and held out his hand to Kelli. "I'm going to go now so that we can each get a good night's sleep. You really must be tired. I can't believe that you had enough energy to stay up half the night after we arrived home last night."

Kelli was following Jace to the door, but stopped and looked at him with a puzzled expression. "What do you mean? I slept like a baby for twelve solid hours."

Jace scratched his head as this statement sunk in. "When I went to bed at around nine last night, I glanced over here and saw that your upstairs light was on. Then I got up during the night and went to the kitchen for a drink and saw that your light was still on. I figured the time difference was playing havoc with your sleep rhythms, and that you decided to do some work in the loft area."

"That's impossible, Jace. I never even went upstairs to the loft last night. And when I went to bed, I made sure that all the lights in the house were off."

Jace studied her face for a long time then rubbed his chin. "I think she's making herself known to you again, Kelli."

"But, if she wants me to see her, then why doesn't she simply appear to me again, just like she used to?"

Jace considered the question for a while, and then simply shrugged. "I don't know. However, I recently remembered that our neighbor Matt, the astronomy professor, is also a member of the Ozark Paranormal Society and has gone on a few of their ghost hunts. If you'd like, we can see if they might be interested in searching your house to find if they can detect anything of significance. I'm sure they would find your history with this house and your connection with seeing the little girl's apparition very appealing."

Kelli thought about this for a minute, and despite her initial negative feeling of having people probing around her house in the dark, she considered the outcome. She chewed on her bottom lip, lost in deep thought, before answering. "It wouldn't hurt anything, I suppose. And it would be nice to find out if she's still here . . . perhaps, what she wants from me."

"I'll give Matt a call tomorrow." He gave her another quick kiss before heading toward the back door. "Now, get some sleep. As for me, I'll go home and try to sleep all alone, no matter how difficult it may be for me."

"Poor baby," Kelli crooned, as she closed the door behind him and locked it. She leaned against it and crossed her arms, smiling broadly and wondering what they had gotten themselves into, and what the future held in store for them.

* * * * * * * *

The rest of the week was a blur as the relaxing days and nights of Zambia were replaced with daily chores, endless decisions, and tons of correspondence now that they were home.

Welcome back to reality, thought Kelli, as she was returning yet another e-mail to Totseui today. It was late evening there, and she imagined Totseui sitting in the makeshift office at the farm. It was nice being able to not only put a face with his name now, but to also visualize the office area and farm that belonged to her.

Kelli had received prices for some equipment that would greatly expand their harvesting procedures. She had already decided to plant the remaining farmland in arabechia plants and would need to be thinking about leasing or purchasing additional land if the demand for this herb proved to be high. She had also made follow-up calls to the management at the manufacturing facility that was interested in handling her harvested product.

Jace had returned to work the day after their dinner with Mrs. Tanner, and she had briefly seen him one time, although they talked by phone on most days when he had a quick break. As he had promised her, he had spoken with Matt and explained the situation to him concerning a ghost expedition in Kelli's house, and Matt had been quick to speak on behalf of the other members in the group.

"A possible haunted house right down the street from me? Who would have ever guessed? Sure, we'll be glad to check it out," he had agreed. "What about this Saturday night? We'll plan to arrive around 8:00 p.m. and begin setting up."

Chapter 16

J ace had been inundated with patients and emergencies this week, often leaving his house before dawn and returning after dark. Even though Dr. Nehow had substituted for him while he was away, his regular patients had chosen to reschedule their appointments upon his return so that they could see their own doctor. This, coupled with the few emergencies and his regularly-scheduled patients, had thrown his work week into a tailspin. By Friday night he was so tired that he fell asleep immediately after getting home and crashing on his bed. He slept hard because when he awoke the next morning, he was in the same facedown position in which he had fallen asleep the night before.

He got up, showered, then dressed in casual shorts and a t-shirt and was about to call Kelli when he glanced out his front window toward her house and saw her in the backyard, filling large patio pots with colorful flowers. He decided to walk over instead.

She saw him approaching her house, his long, toned legs making serious strides. She put her trowel down, stood up straight, and met him with a kiss. "Hi, stranger. I've missed you."

"Tell me that again," he said, giving her another kiss.

"Talk about a long week. I'll remember to expect that the next time I take off on a vacation." He nodded to the filled pots sitting around the patio. "Nice job. It really makes your patio appealing," he praised.

"Thanks. Are you hungry?" she asked, removing her gardening gloves.

"Starved. And I suppose for some food, too," he quipped.

"Wise guy." She shot him a look and pointed to the chair. "Have a seat at the patio table and I'll be right back."

Kelli returned a moment later carrying a tray of freshly baked blueberry muffins and two stoneware mugs of steaming coffee.

"You are a true angel, Kelli. What time did you get up to have all this done? Dawn?"

"No," she laughed aloud. "But I guessed that you would be hungry. Did you sleep well?"

"Like a log. I still have creases in my face from sleeping facedown for twelve hours to prove it." He pointed to the side of his face and she laughed.

"These are delicious," Jace said in between bites of his second muffin. "So, are you ready for the paranormal society to arrive tonight at your house?"

Kelli looked away. "I guess so."

Jace instantly caught the hesitancy in her voice. "What's wrong?"

"Nothing. Well, okay, maybe I have some reservations about the reputability of it all. Plus, it almost seems wrong to have strangers probing around my house trying to find . . . her."

"Come here," Jace said, chuckling, as he took her in his arms. "Nothing will happen to 'her'. Let's just hope that, if we are lucky, we can validate her existence in the house."

"By the way," he said, raising an eyebrow in her direction, "it will be nearly impossible for you to get any sleep in your house unless you plan to stay up and follow the group around all night. So, I think the best thing for you would be to stay at my house tonight."

"Hmmm, I assume those are the doctor's orders?" teased Kelli.

"You bet they are," he smiled, leaning over to squeeze her tightly.

Just at that moment a rustle was heard in the side yard, and Mrs. Tanner emerged from the pruned hedges separating her yard from Kelli's. As she spotted them in an embrace, a huge smile spread over her face. Nothing could please this matchmaker more.

She joined them on the patio and even shared a blueberry muffin. She, too, had seen Kelli filling the flower pots earlier and wanted to come see them up close. The three of them shared a half hour of easy conversation, and as Kelli watched Mrs. Tanner and Jace speaking, a sense of well-being overcame her as she realized that more than twenty years before, the three of them had shared many such visits, of a more juvenile nature, of course. She was again reminded of her decision to return to this neighborhood and felt that she had undeniably made the correct choice.

The rest of the day was filled with errands and chores. The house was tidied up, and Kelli was ready when the doorbell rang around 8:00 that night.

"It's show time," she muttered under her breath, as if coaxing the house's ghost to cooperate.

Jace had met the eclectic group as they were emerging from their vehicles and escorted them to the front door. Kelli was thankful that some sort of vehicle bearing a huge logo of the ghost-hunting group was not parked outside her house, giving the neighbors something to gossip about.

Once inside, introductions were made by Matt, and the group of five young men asked Kelli a few questions related to what made her speculate that her house may be haunted. She relayed the story from her childhood to the group who sat in wide-eyed amazement as they listened. They rarely were asked to perform tests on a house with so much repetitive history and were quite optimistic that some sort of energy would be detected that night.

Matt and a young man named Jaden showed Kelli and Jace the equipment they brought along. As Matt unzipped a large bag, Jaden

141

brought out a digital recorder and explained that this piece of equipment was needed to record electronic voice phenomena. An EMF meter was also passed around as Jaden explained that this device was used to locate electromagnetic fields, with the theory being that the presence of ghosts might disrupt this field. Another device they brought was a thermal scanner to locate cold spots, since ghosts can drain warmth from air. "However," cautioned Jaden, "cold spots can have all sorts of causes, and locating one does not automatically mean that it is caused by a ghost."

"Don't forget this basic item," chimed in Matt, as he lifted a digital camera from another bag. "This, along with that video recorder over there, can record pictures that we can later look at on the computer and sometimes find things that we may have earlier missed."

After the guys unpacked their equipment, Kelli showed them around the house, including the newer loft area upstairs. She had supplied soft drinks, a pitcher of tea, and some sandwiches for them in the kitchen and encouraged them to help themselves throughout the night. She and Jace watched the group set up and test the equipment, before they explained that Kelli would be staying across the road at Jace's house for the remainder of the night. Most of the recording would begin closer to midnight and would last until dawn. Kelli promised the group that she would be back at that hour to see what they had found, and encouraged them to call her cell if they needed anything.

As Jace and Kelli stepped outside, the summer night air was still quite warm and balmy, heavy with the humidity well-known to Southerners. Darkness was just beginning to descend, although the night insects were already chirping in synchronized harmony. An Arkansas summer evening such as this was one of the things she so desperately missed while living and working up North.

There was something about being caressed by the heaviness of the air, warm but no longer hot, accompanied by all the various sounds and smells of a summer night, which made everything about her life feel right.

Taking Jace's hand, they walked through her back yard and across the road to his house.

When they arrived at his place, rather than going inside, Jace surprised her by leading her around behind the house to the patio that was now enveloped by low-hanging branches of elm trees. A small wrought iron table was covered in a checkered tablecloth, and sitting on top of it was a bottle of wine chilling in a silver bucket. A plate of black grapes, assorted cheeses and crackers, and two wine glasses were arranged beside it.

Kelli abruptly stopped walking and laid a hand on her chest. "Oh, Jace . . . how lovely," she whispered.

He was still holding her hand, watching her pleased reaction, before spinning her around to face him. He tilted her head up to look into his eyes, and when he spoke his voice with thick with emotion.

"I love you, Kelli. I want to make you happy, even by doing little things such as this." He lowered his head and kissed her with a passion and tenderness that reflected their past, their reconnection, their future. He pulled back and sighed, holding her cheek against his own for a moment, before clasping her hand, and kissing her again. They stood in an embrace for several minutes, and each knew how the other felt, although not a word had been spoken.

By now dusk had been completely replaced with darkness, and overhead a half moon had emerged in the inky, eastern night sky. They sat at the table, and each shared snippets of their week: funny anecdotes, the difficulty of returning to work after a long vacation, and their recollections of Zambia. Kelli filled Jace in on her conversations with Totseui throughout the week.

Soon, their conversation turned to the ghost-hunting group in Kelli's house, wondering if anything would be discovered.

Jace sat back in his chair, with his arms crossed in front of his chest, a finger pressed against his lips.

Kelli knew that look. "What are you thinking, Jace?"

"Remember that grave at the edge of the woods down the road a bit?"

"Yes, of course. It is what caused me to think about the possibility of it being connected to the apparition when I was small."

"Yes. And all we knew about it as children was that it belonged to the grave of a young girl." He suddenly sat up straight in the chair. "Why haven't we thought to check it out before now?" He was already standing up, pushing in his chair.

"What are you doing?" Kelli asked, not quite sure if she was ready to admit the fact that she clearly understood he wanted to investigate it at this very minute in the darkness of night.

"Come on. I'll grab a flashlight."

"But, it's dark," Kelli argued.

"Now's as good a time as any."

Although Kelli could have easily argued that last statement, she found herself walking alongside Jace at a quick pace on the road that led to the grave. In an easy five minutes they reached the sloped edge of the wooded hillside, which now eerily loomed straight above them in the darkness.

Jace shone the light toward the tree line in an attempt to remember where the grave was located. After all, it had been almost two decades since they had last seen it as children.

Kelli looked around at all the shadows playing off the trees and shuddered. "I don't know about this, Jace."

"Come on, you're not chicken are you?" He was trying to needle her, and she knew it.

"Couldn't this wait until daylight? I mean, it reminds me of when we played 'Truth or Dare,' and one of us would dare the other to walk down the road in the dark." She snickered. "No one ever made it very far."

Jace laughed at the memory as he tried to remember where the little grave sat. "We used to have to walk a little way into the woods somewhere about right here," he was murmuring as much to himself as to Kelli. "However, the road has been widened over the years, so we'll need to adjust for that."

He shone the light to the right and scanned slowly over to the left, stopping to focus on a thicket of brambles amid fallen logs.

"I think this is it!" he announced with excitement in his voice. "Come on, follow me."

Kelli didn't need much prodding to stay with him. Her only other choice would be to stand alone out here in the creepy darkness.

Jace reached back for her hand and helped her over the logs, holding back the overgrown, thorny vines and errant limbs that threatened to snatch and trip them. They walked a little farther, and then they saw it at the same time—a solitary, faded, small tombstone jutting out of the rocky hillside. Pitching sharply to the left, it appeared practically forgotten, lost in a wild tangle of wayward honeysuckle vines and wild privet.

Jace reached it first and knelt down to feel the cool smoothness of the old stone. "Let's see if we can read the inscription."

But as he shone the flashlight directly onto the stone's surface, they quickly saw that whatever had once been inscribed was now worn so smooth that most of it was no longer legible.

"We won't be able to discover anything from this," Kelli said despondently. "We can't even read it."

"Not so fast," Jace said. "I've read that you can perform rubbings on old tombstones and sometimes retrieve the inscription that way." He was already turning back toward the road. "I'll run and grab a piece of paper and a pencil."

"I'm coming with you. There's no way you are leaving me here all alone while you are gone," Kelli warned, jumping ahead of him.

"Chicken?" Jace goaded, sounding much again like the ten-year old boy that gained extreme enjoyment from teasing her.

"Yes, and I'm not afraid to admit it. If you leave me here, you'd better plan on performing an emergency heart surgery tonight—on me." Kelli grabbed Jace by the arm, and together they quickly walked the short distance to his house.

After retrieving a paper and pencil, they returned to the tombstone. By now the moon was shining brightly overhead, and the trees cast long, ghoulish-looking shadows across the road, causing Kelli to keep looking over her shoulder.

She held the flashlight for Jace as he again knelt down, this time gently placing the paper over the stone. He then held the pencil at various angles until he found one that worked and lightly rubbed it over the paper. He soon began to make out a few letters.

"It looks like the name began with an 'F' or an 'S,' and somewhere in the name appears to be an 'E.'" He continued rubbing across the headstone, not being able to make out much of anything else until he got to the last letter. "I'm pretty sure that the name ended with an 'R,'" he confirmed.

Next, he moved down to the dates, and although he discovered that the birth month was in September, he couldn't make out the year. But he excitedly was able to uncover the death date—March 1914.

146

"Nowhere on this stone do we find a first name," said Jace, scratching his temple.

"But when we were nosy kids," began Kelli, "we were told that the grave belonged to a young girl. So our parents must've have heard that from somewhere."

Jace turned to her. "Remember the family's name who originally owned your house, Kelli?"

She knew the name, had known it all her life. "The Schroeders." As soon as she said it, she realized where Jace was leading her. "Shroeder" began with an "S," had an "E" in it and ended with an "R."

"Bingo," he muttered.

Kelli let out a long, slow sigh. When she had grown older, she wondered if the night apparition of the little girl and the lone grave down the road were connected. It now most certainly appeared that they were.

Chapter 17

I t was almost five in the morning when Kelli quietly slipped out of Jace's house and headed to her own across the road. Jace was still sleeping and looked so peaceful that she hadn't had the heart to wake him. After they had returned to his house last night, he fixed coffee and sat with her for hours while she talked. She needed a friend, a confidante, someone who understood her. And when she had finished talking, he had taken her in his arms and loved her with such tenderness and intensity that it had touched something deep inside the core of her being.

At her house all five men, including Matt, were beginning to pack up their equipment and supplies when Kelli walked in the back door. "Hello guys, how did it go last night?" she asked, searching their eyes for some sign of success.

Matt drained the last of the Pepsi in his can before answering. "Nothing out of the ordinary; however, we found a particularly higher than normal reading on the thermal scanner in one specific area of the house."

Kelli knew instantly the specific area of the house in which he was referring. She felt goose bumps prickle her flesh as he added, "It was in the kitchen."

It had been an hour now since the group had left, promising to call her if they found anything on their recorder and camera when they viewed it later that day. They would analyze all tapes and listen to all recordings once they got back to their office.

Kelli was sitting at the kitchen table second-guessing her decision and still wondering if she had done the right thing by having the group probe around her house. It was almost as if she felt she was violating the dignity of her house's ghost, who had befriended her so long ago. She had brought in strangers with recorders and machines, trying to pick up the vibes of someone who had been peacefully—and anonymously—residing here for decades. What right did she have to disturb her existence?

She sighed heavily and decided then and there that she would not initiate any future paranormal searches. The sanctity of her home would be preserved from here on. Whoever resided here with her would remain a welcome habitant of the house, as well.

She heard a soft knock at the back door, followed by Jace's voice.

"Good morning, anybody here?"

She rose to greet him. "Just me. The group left about an hour ago." She stood on tiptoe to give him a kiss, and he wrapped his arms around her.

"You were gone when I woke up. Why didn't you wake me?"

"I couldn't do it. You were so patient listening to me rattle on last night. I didn't mean to keep you up that late."

He squeezed her tighter. "Patience had nothing to do with it. I'm flattered you wanted to share your thoughts with me, Kelli, and I'll always be here to listen. Remember that."

As she stood enveloped in his strong embrace with her head on his shoulder, she knew without a doubt that he was speaking the truth.

After a little cajoling from Kelli, they spent the afternoon browsing flooring at local stores, getting some ideas for his house. All Jace decided was that he wanted hardwood, and he left all the details on style, color, and durability to Kelli who loved making choices such as these. While she had him out, they also looked at paint colors. She was trying to get a hint at what colors he favored, but again, he wanted to leave these choices entirely to her.

They decided to watch a movie at Jace's house that night. Kelli prepared a salad, while Jace grilled a couple steaks, and they shared a bottle of wine over dinner. It was a relaxing way to end such a long and harried week.

* * * * * * * *

When Mr. Mills arrived on Monday morning, Kelli was already at work painting the guest bedroom.

"Mornin." He tipped the bill of his cap at her. "I see you don't let any grass grow under your feet," he joked, while watching her paint the room he'd just completed on Friday. He picked up his hammer and the bag of nails sitting on the floor. "I'd better hurry in this little half-bath because I don't think there's room for the two of us to work in here at the same time." His eyes crinkled as he smiled at her and his voice held humor. "Besides, if I'm not careful, you're apt to put a coat of paint over me."

Kelli laughed at his bantering and then shot him a smug look. "You know how I get when I have a paint brush in my hand," she warned.

The two of them chatted easily for the rest of the morning as they worked. Kelli had grown to admire Mr. Mills for his work ethic, his beautiful workmanship, and for his honesty. He had asked her many questions pertaining to Zambia when she'd returned and he'd confided that he had never before traveled further than the bordering states.

Jace stopped by on the way home from work later that evening to see how the final rooms of the renovation were progressing. While he was there, Matt called.

"Hi, Kelli. I just wanted to let you know that nothing terribly significant was found on the video recorder. We did see some type of image, but it was grainy and hard to decipher. When we replayed the film frame-by-frame, we couldn't tell much of anything, whether we were seeing a male or female, young or old. It just appeared out of nowhere, and a few frames later, it disappeared."

"Where was this image located?" Kelli asked, but she already knew the answer before he spoke.

"In the middle of the kitchen." He paused a moment before he continued. "We all agreed that there is some sort of energy in your home. If you'd like, we can schedule another night to come back. We can set up specifically in the kitchen area and see if we can learn more."

Kelli didn't have to consider this for long. She didn't want to put herself or her friendly ghost through any additional intrusions in the future. "No thanks, but I do appreciate your coming to check things out. It reinforced what I already knew. Please thank the rest of the group for me."

As Matt started to hang up, he thought of something else. "Oh, there's one more thing, Kelli. The audio recorder caught a peculiar sound at some point during the night. We all listened to it repeatedly and decided that it sounded like the beat of hooves, perhaps those of cattle or horses. It was quite strange because we usually don't pick up on animal sounds."

Kelli thought this was unusual and after she hung up, she relayed the conversation to Jace who had been listening by her side.

"I'm not surprised you don't want to undergo another ghost hunt. I know you weren't too fond of the idea in the first place." He looked remorseful. "In fact, I regret ever suggesting it to you."

"Don't be, Jace. I'll admit I was reluctant, but I was also curious, as well. I did learn something, though."

"What's that?"

"Not only do I have a ghost to contend with, but now I have to be listening for horses in my house." They both shared a laugh and let the subject drop.

* * * * * * *

By Thursday, Mr. Mills had finished the final two rooms downstairs, and now all that was left was for the plumber to connect the water in the small guest bathroom. Kelli had applied two coats of paint in both rooms and was eager to furnish the guestroom. And she was happy with her final decision to make the upstairs loft area a library. Considering that books would need shelves, she had asked Mr. Mills if he could build a couple of simple bookcases up there as a last project.

He seemed pleased to do so and began planning the most aesthetically-pleasing way to construct them. On the interior wall which separated the attic from the loft area, he'd thought of a way to create a built-in unit, without sacrificing square footage. He measured and planned to cut out an opening in the wall and recess the bookcase into the attic wall. On the adjoining wall, he'd hoped to be able to the same, even though he would be cutting into the wall which comprised the exterior side of the house.

He was cutting out a large portion from this outer wall, when he made the discovery.

Something caught his eye through the cloud of particleboard dust that filled the air. He waited for the dust to settle before moving closer to inspect it, and then reached into the dark recess behind the wall. His fingers grasped the corner of some object, but it wouldn't budge. Using gentle force, he tried a different angle and this time he succeeded. He pulled out some sort of ancient-looking, leather-bound book.

He blew away the dust as he looked at the worn cover. "Hey, Kelli," he called down. "Come look at what I just found!"

Kelli walked to the bottom of the stairs and looked up. "What is it?" she cautiously asked, half-expecting him to have found a dead rat, or worse, a live snake.

"Just come take a look."

* * * * * * * *

She had spent the last few hours poring over the carefully written entries of what appeared to be a diary belonging to Frank A. Shroeder. He had been a prolific writer and recorded many entries in his journal, documenting the various hardships and triumphs of life in this small town in the late 1800's and early 1900's. Kelli felt that this manuscript belonged in a museum, for it provided such a detailed account of everyday life during this era. Descriptions of the old town square, including the general mercantile store and the local blacksmith shop, were given. There was even a crudely-drawn map of the town in its early days.

Captivated by his entries, Kelli read some that caused her to smile.

May 25, 1908:

Today my sweetheart, Nora Rae, became my wedded wife. I consider myself the luckiest man alive. We've known each other since we were young-uns, since we grew up on adjoining farms. Her pa actually helped mine with his barn-raising and her ma assisted my ma in my sister's birth. Our first date was a little under a year ago when I asked her to the town's annual square dance on the Fourth of July.

Our wedding was just the way she wanted it—plain and simple. We married in a field of wildflowers at sundown and she wore her ma's wedding dress and carried fresh-picked daisies. When we said our vows, there was a light breeze that ruffled her pretty golden hair and at that moment I was sure that I'd never met anyone more beautiful. I pray that we will share many, many happy days together in the years to come.

Kelli closed her eyes and imagined this young couple standing in a field at sunset long ago as they were united as husband and wife. She was eager to read the accounts in the years to follow to find if theirs was a long and happy union as he had so desperately wanted. She kept reading account after account and learning about the life and family of this couple.

September 2, 1909:

Today is the first day that Nora will serve as teacher in the one-room schoolhouse down the road. She was pretty excited this morning when she woke up and packed her lunch. She's wanted to teach since she was a little girl and today her dream will come true.

Mr. Mills had sat at the kitchen table with her for a while after he found the diary, and together they read entry after entry, marveling at the history recorded in such detailed accounts. He had left her house a couple hours earlier, but Kelli still remained at the kitchen table, lost in the long-ago tales of Mr. Shroeder.

The recorded entries were so captivating and clearly-written that she felt as if she had traveled back in time as she experienced what life must have been like for this family. She read of happy times, as well as hard times, and learned about all the difficulties of living during this period.

She was reading a March 1914 entry when she felt like she had been struck by a bolt of lightning. A cold chill traveled up her spine, and something akin to fear gripped her heart and wouldn't let go. For a long moment she couldn't breathe, and then she began weeping as she reread the words that were penned in ink so long ago.

She was shaking and sobbing uncontrollably when she picked up her phone and dialed Jace's number. His voice mail promptly came on, indicating that he was most likely still at work.

Her message was succinct, though her voice was hardly recognizable through the sobs. "Come over when you get home tonight, Jace. I believe our mystery is solved."

Chapter 18

I t was a little after nine that night when Jace left the hospital's cardiology wing. He had been there since early afternoon performing a triple-bypass on a 79-year-old patient. Everything had gone well, the patient was recovering nicely, but he was exhausted from being on his feet for the past several hours. His eyes burned and the muscles in his neck were sore and tight from being bent over the operating table for so long.

As he reached his car in the parking lot, he checked his phone messages. When he heard Kelli's strained voice on the first message, he had to play it again to be sure he understood what she had said. She sounded terribly upset over something, and he found himself driving well above the legal speed limit in order to reach her house quickly.

He wheeled into her driveway while simultaneously opening his car door and had his foot on the ground before his car had come to a complete stop. He ran to the back of the house, near the kitchen, where he had a feeling he would find her. He knocked briefly on the back door, then checked the door knob and found it to be unlocked. He had barely stepped inside when Kelli ran to him and threw her arms around him.

"What is it, Kel? What's wrong?" He was desperate to find out what was troubling her. Prying her arms from his neck, he looked into her eyes which were puffy and red from crying. He led her to the couch, sat down beside her, and then encouraged her to tell him what was upsetting her.

Kelli took a deep breath and then slowly began talking. "Mr. Mills was upstairs constructing a pair of built-in bookcases in the loft area. When he knocked a hole in the wall, he found this." She got up and went to the table to retrieve the diary and handed it to Jace.

He stared at it in his hands for a long moment, wondering how this innocent-looking, little book could possibly be the cause for her distress.

"What is it, an old bookkeeping ledger?" he wondered aloud, before opening its fragile cover.

"Go ahead and see for yourself," Kelli urged.

Jace carefully opened it and read the first page which stated that the book was a diary belonging to Frank A. Shroeder, of Fayetteville, Arkansas.

He glanced over at Kelli, before turning the next few pages and reading the entries. "This is a fascinating history, Kelli," he said, after he read a few pages, still clueless as to why she was so upset.

"Turn to the year 1914, and look for the entry dated March 11," instructed Kelli, with more calm in her voice than she felt.

Jace did so, and as he began quietly reading the entry aloud, he quickly discovered the cause of Kelli's grief.

March 11, 1914:

Today was a mighty sad day for the family. We buried my eight-year old niece, Sara Evelyn Shroeder in a plot of land that my brother wants to make into a family cemetery. It is situated in the middle of some woods where Sara used to play with her dolls. I don't know if my brother, who is her father, will ever get over her death. I am real worried over him, as he has not spoken to anybody and his face now has a permanent wretched look. He is blaming himself for her death, though no one could have controlled the stubborn mules that were pulling the wagon that backed up and pinned her between it and the barn wall.

This is not the first time our family has ever buried a child, but most of the others died either shortly after birth or after only a few months of life. Never have we put to rest a child that died in a horrible accident like this. She was such a lovely child with her long brown hair and blue eyes. Her heart was so pure and she held such a love for all of God's creatures. Her ma sewed a burial dress for her out of the navy material that little Sarah had picked out at the general store just last week. She wanted a new dress and we never dreamt that she would end up being buried in it. In my mind I will forever see her little body in that casket, looking for all the world like a little angel. We buried her with her favorite doll in her arms. It made us feel better knowing that we weren't going to be lowering her into that cold, dark ground all alone. Course, we all know that she is not actually in the ground because her soul is with our Heavenly Father. It is still too much to bear and our family is all torn up over it. I pray to our Father that he heals us real quick-like and grants some peace to our souls and that he takes good care of little Sara 'til we all get there to see her again someday.

Jace finished reading and silently looked over at Kelli who was sitting stoically with fresh tears streaming down her cheeks.

"It's her, Jace. It's been her all along. She was buried in a navy dress and holding a doll, which is how the apparition appeared to me at night when I was a little girl. Now I know her name—Sara Evelyn Shroeder."

Jace was lost in his own thoughts, his mind still reeling from what he'd just read. "March 1914 is the date that is inscribed on the tombstone at the edge of the clearing," he whispered. "So, it does appear to be her, for sure."

"And now we know that she was eight years old," Kelli said in a hushed voice.

"What a tragic death, Kelli. She was crushed by a wagon pulled by mules . . . ."

"The sound of hooves!" Kelli cried, as a new thought surfaced. "The sound of beating hooves that were heard inside my house on the audio recorder must have been of those mules."

She lowered her head into her hands. "Oh, Jace, this is so much to comprehend at once."

Jace scooted his chair closer to Kelli and wrapped her in his arms. Together they grieved for a little girl they had never met, but one who had been a part of their childhood just the same. For Kelli, Sara had appeared to her on numerous occasions. For both of them, visiting her lone tombstone in the woods as children had been a place that represented uncertainty, even fear. There was much speculation about who the grave belonged to and what had happened to the little girl buried there. Now because of the entry in Frank Shroeder's diary, the answer was provided.

As Kelli had read the diary's pages, she realized that she would never look at this community in the same way anymore, but would remember the hard work and sacrifices it took to become what it is today. She also gained a fresh perspective for the rolling hills and pastures surrounding her house, knowing others from generations before her had loved and raised families and lived rich lives on the exact same land.

Jace didn't think she needed to stay alone that night considering her state of mind, so she stayed at his house, wrapped in his strong, comforting arms throughout the night. When he left for his early-morning rounds at the hospital in the morning, she returned to her house.

She was apprehensive as she walked in the back door, unsure if she would be met with a new atmosphere—one of hesitation and even laced with a tinge of fright. To her relief, this didn't happen, yet she sensed a subtle difference. Perhaps it was simply closure.

Mr. Mills returned later that morning, ready to complete the bookshelves in the loft.

"That journal was quite a find yesterday. Did you learn anything more from it?" he asked Kelli, seeming extremely pleased to have uncovered such a treasure.

She thought to herself that there was no way he could ever begin to know how much she learned. Instead she smiled and answered, "I certainly gained an appreciation for the people who lived here and worked this land."

He could never possibly understand what finding the journal and the answer it held had meant to her.

* * * * * * * *

On Saturday late morning Jace showed up at Kelli's back door and invited her to take a walk with him.

Kelli jumped at the suggestion and sat down to put on her shoes. "Where are we going?" she asked.

He offered a small smile. "You'll see."

He had brought along a large bag and she followed him through the backyard and out to the road.

"What have you got in there?" she curiously asked.

"You'll see."

They began walking down the road and Kelli quickly sensed where they were headed. "We're going to her grave, aren't we?"

His voice was tight, his words a little clipped. "Yes. There's something we need to do."

By now they had reached the edge of the woods, and Jace again led the way through the riot of brambles, vines, and fallen logs. The little tombstone didn't appear eerie in the daytime, just lonely and forlorn, thought Kelli. Perhaps it could simply be attributed to the fact that the mystery of the old grave had been uncovered, its story now told.

"I thought she deserved a little respect," Jace began, as he opened the bag and took out a pair of loppers and pruners. He handed the pruners to Kelli, and then he began cutting away the tangled mass of vines that threatened to entirely cover the portion of the headstone that protruded. She followed suit, snipping away the thorny vines that encompassed the area.

"Frank Shroeder wrote that his brother wanted to make this a family cemetery," Kelli said, as she worked. "But I don't see any more graves here. I wonder what happened."

"We'll probably never know why," Jace answered. "Unless we find another diary someday. But, I'm not holding my breath waiting for that to happen."

He pulled down a thick, twisted, wild grapevine that hung from high in a treetop directly above the grave, allowing a small beam of golden sunlight to penetrate the thick canopy of the forest and spotlight the headstone. "After I went to bed last night I kept thinking about this little neglected grave sitting all alone at the edge of the woods. It is basically lost and unknown in today's world. But, Sara was someone's daughter, someone's sister, someone who was once very much loved. It saddens me that she is now forgotten."

He grunted as he firmly pushed the old headstone back to an upright position and packed more dirt around its base. "Then I started thinking that you and I know that she is buried here. We know her story. I realized that the responsibility has fallen on us to remember and honor her."

He opened the bag again and reached inside. "That's why I brought this," he said, as he retrieved a beautiful wreath made of delicate pink, silk flowers and woven with frilly burgundy ribbons. Threaded through the

161

middle was a petite, white satin, sequined banner which simply read, *Not Forgotten.*

As Jace carefully placed the pretty wreath on the little tombstone, a strangled sob escaped Kelli's throat. He came over to stand beside her and wrapped an arm around her shoulders.

"You are the kindest and most honorable man I have ever met, and I love you so very much," Kelli said, choking on her words and hugging him tightly.

She didn't have to tell him this for he could read it in her expression and see it reflected in her eyes. She could no more hide her love for him than he could hide his for her. Still, he always longed to hear it from her lips, as he just had.

He squeezed her a little harder and whispered in her ear, "I love you, too, Kelli."

It was while standing at the small grave, wrapped in Jace's strong arms, that Kelli knew without a doubt she wanted to spend the rest of her life with this man. He represented everything meaningful in her life: her past, her present, and now Kelli knew that he was also destined to share her future. She would forever treasure their strong bond of friendship that was forged in childhood, for it was a lasting bond. But now she knew she equally cherished this new bond that had emerged and taken hold of their hearts.

Chapter 19

A couple of weeks had passed since the Saturday morning they had walked to Sara's grave and Jace had placed the wreath on it. Jace had been extremely busy back at the clinic, and Kelli stayed equally busy with all the paperwork concerning her farm and reaching potential clients. Mr. Mills had completely finished the remodeling work at Kelli's house and after paying him, she promised to call him whenever she had any additional carpentry work that might occur. "In the meantime," she had told him, "you better stop by and say hello to me on a regular basis. I always have a pitcher of sweet tea in my refrigerator."

His smile had spread from ear to ear when she told him this, and he was pleased that she liked his finished work.

"You practically have yourself a new home," he remarked. "But seeing how it was your old home place and all, I guess you can never achieve that sentimental feeling by building a new house."

"No you can't, and I plan to own this one forever."

She had meant it when she said it. Should she ever move into another house during her lifetime, she planned to somehow keep this one in the family. It meant too much to her, and she knew that after getting it back for a second time in life, she could never part with it again.

She was catching up on some paperwork in her upstairs library one morning when the manager of a pharmaceutical lab in London called her. They had performed extensive lab tests regarding the potential healing properties of the arabechia herb and were extremely interested to give it a trial run. Her farm was listed as one of the few who were currently growing this herb, and they wanted to order a shipment when it was harvested.

Kelli was absolutely elated when she hung up the phone. She had tried to remain calm and sound like the cool and collected businesswoman she imagined herself to be, but deep inside she was screaming with excitement. Her business investment just might pay off one day.

Still, she knew there was loads of work to be done, but her next move was to call Totseui and inform him about the London lab. She dialed his phone number and heard the ringing followed by a click as he answered on the other side of the world. She was always amazed at what could be done using today's technology.

"Totseui, it's Kelli," she began. "Sorry to bother you after hours. Am I interrupting anything?"

"Not at all, I'm still in office finishing paperwork," he answered, in his charming broken English.

She mentally offered a prayer of thanks for having a diligent and hard-working manager such as him. "You are keeping late hours," she noted. "But, wait till you hear what I have to tell you."

She relayed the good news to him, trying to speak slowly and concisely, but catching herself gushing with excitement and having to repeat herself a few times. Totseui laughed out loud and seemed genuinely pleased, and they again talked about the need to begin negotiations on leasing additional farmland to grow more arabechia. All of this meant more jobs for the locals, and both Kelli and Totseui were thrilled.

She couldn't wait to share the news with Jace. When they talked that evening after work, he was so thrilled for her and had insisted on taking her out the next evening for a fabulous celebratory dinner at a very nice restaurant. After dinner he told her that he needed some extra design ideas regarding his house and asked if she could meet him at the site the next morning, which was Saturday.

So here she was, climbing the hillside on her way to meet Jace at the house site. The builders had been steadily working, and Kelli was extremely pleased to see what all had been completed. She walked around the first floor, but it appeared she was alone. Unsure if Jace had arrived yet, she called out his name.

"Up here, Kel," she heard him answer. "In the Enemy Lookout Tower Room."

She smiled at the name, glad that at her suggestion he had decided to dub the room by that name and climbed the stairs to find him. Through the open framework of studs, she could see him sitting in a chair.

"What are you doing up there?" she asked curiously.

A smile teased the corners of his mouth. "Waiting for you."

She climbed the last few steps a little apprehensively and stepped into the room. The patio table and two chairs had been hauled up here and Jace, who had been sitting in one, now rose to greet her.

"What in the world?" Kelli began, looking around her at the table and chairs. It had taken some work to get them up here.

He greeted her with a kiss and then pulled her chair out for her. "I thought we could talk here," he said, as he pulled out a box that was filled with samples of paint strips and flooring squares.

Kelli thought it was rather odd, but scooted her chair in closer as he continued. "I want you to tell me what colors you recommend in this room." He handed her the box.

With a quizzical expression on her face, Kelli picked out a sample and began to unroll it.

Jace was watching her. "I was thinking of a darker color, more like the one on the sample underneath."

Kelli reached in and pulled out that particular sample which was tightly rolled and held in place with something. She started to pull the paper out, but suddenly saw what was holding it so securely. She gasped and clutched at her heart as she realized that it was a sparkling diamond ring. She looked over at Jace who was solemnly watching her reaction with a mix of tenderness and love shining in his eyes.

He rose from his seat, walked to her, and pulled her into his arms. Looking deeply into her eyes he spoke the words that she now realized she had been longing to hear for a long time.

"Kelli, I can't imagine not having you in my life. Though our relationship has changed over time, it began many years ago with our deep friendship. I believe that you were meant to return so that we could be together forever."

He dropped to one knee. "I love you with all of my heart, Kelli. Please say that you will marry me."

By now Kelli was crying tears of pure joy as she looked down at Jace who was still balanced on one knee in front of her. She fully grasped the fact that they were inevitably destined to be together, and in her heart of hearts she knew that he had always been the only one for her. Fate had worked its magic to bring them together again. An indiscernible, yet powerful, bond to her childhood house, and ultimately to this man, had brought her back to this town.

She had come full circle and was currently back in the place where she had started, but now with a future full of endless promises. This is where she was meant to be, and these arms were the ones that were meant to hold her, she realized as her lips met his.

"Yes, Jace. Oh, yes," she whispered between kisses.

Epilogue

7 Years Later

It was well past midnight, and Kelli was hard at work in her office speaking via Skype with the purchasing director of an overseas medical lab. It was necessary to work late into the night on some occasions because of the time differences of her clients who lived in other parts of the world. However, now that she had an assistant to help with the paperwork and answer the phone, her days were mostly free.

After she disconnected, she sat at her desk which was located in the former living room of her childhood home. Jace had been the one who had actually suggested using the house as an office for her burgeoning arabechia business. That way, she would get to be in it every day, and it was a short walk from their home on the hill across the road.

Her business had taken off exponentially since that first call she had received seven years ago from the lab in London. They were still a huge client, but other labs in other countries, including America, had heard about her farm, one of the first which began commercially growing arabechia, and contacted her with orders. Never had she dreamed that this business would take off as it had, but she was grateful that she had followed her instinct and made the initial investment.

Kelli and Jace had returned to Zambia many times. Totseui was still at the original farm in Zambia, but he had been promoted to the company's vice president and oversaw the added managers who had been hired to oversee the hundreds of additional acres of arabechia which had been planted following the explosive surge of interest in the herb.

Neither could she have ever dreamed that she would be happily married to the friend she had so often played with as a child.

They were married the following spring, one year after her return to Arkansas, and chose May 25 to be their wedding date in honor of Frank and Nora Shroeder's wedding date. Likewise, their ceremony took place in a field of beautiful wildflowers on the hillside beside the house that Jace built overlooking her beloved childhood home and the lush, rolling hills of the Ozark Mountains beyond.

Who knows? Perhaps it was the same field that Frank and Nora had stood in as they recited their marriage vows so many years before. Jace and Kelli had been surrounded by their family, friends, and of course, Mrs. Tanner, who had cried happy tears throughout most of the ceremony. Kelli couldn't prove it, but she liked to think that perhaps members of the Shroeder family had been present in spirit, as well.

Life is full of twists and turns, an inevitable maze of choices, she thought to herself. Call it fate or chance, but she was happy with the path she had chosen and the way her life had turned out.

She looked over and smiled contentedly at her ten-month old son, Kade, sleeping soundly in the baby bed beside her desk. He had his father's grey eyes and sweet temperament. He and his four-year-old sister Sara were the light of her life. They often spent the night in the house when Jace was on call at the hospital, and Kelli had work to do. It did Kelli's heart good to see her own children sleeping in the same house that she had grown up in and loved so dearly.

A few moments later Kelli's reverie was broken by Sara's sleepy voice calling to her.

"Honey, mommy's in here," Kelli softly answered. She rose and walked around her desk at the same time that Sara was coming down the short hallway. Kelli stood waiting with open arms as Sara hurried to her. However, when her daughter reached the little area that intersected the

www.ingramcontent.com/pod-product-compliance
Lightning Source LLC
Chambersburg PA
CBHW071249130626
46556CB00003B/1235

hallway and the kitchen, she stopped briefly and looked into the kitchen. A smile spread over her face, and she waved happily before scampering along toward her mother's waiting arms.

Kelli's heart quickened. Had Sara just seen the little ghost girl who had so frequently appeared in the night at the very same spot to Kelli when she was young?

Surprisingly, Kelli was comfortable with this probability and strangely, even embraced it. She knew that the Sara born in 1906, and her daughter's namesake, was still with them. Perhaps now she served as a guardian angel over the children of the little girl she had befriended so many years before in the same house.